Wild Sweeps the Wind

A novel based on the real life Civil War diary
of Phebe F. Beach, Esquire

Caroline Grimm

Caroline D. Grimm

DEDICATION

For Cynthia Grimm who freely shares all her gifts with me, including her greatest gift, her daughter. And if she had a tiny dwarf with a red hat, she'd surely share that, too.

ACKNOWLEDGMENTS

I am indebted to the knowledge, kindness, and enthusiasm of a number of people in the writing of this book. First on the list are my friends Herb and Jean Farnsworth. They opened their home to me and drove me into Cambridge each day so I could focus on reading Phebe Beach's diary rather than on the frustrations of traffic and parking. I want to give special mention to my sister, friend, and editor, Cynthia Grimm, "The Comma-dore," for her support and enthusiasm for this project and for once again making my writing skills look far better than they really are. Many thanks to my assistant, Kathy Goughenour, who helps me keep all the balls in the air. A gracious thank you to the pastor and congregation of the South Bridgton Congregational Church for sharing this journey with me.

I want to especially thank the board and members of the Bridgton Historical Society for their dedication to preserving the history of the town that was once called Pondicherry. In particular, thank you to Ned Allen and Kathleen Forsythe Vincent for helping me with accessing the many local resources available. Julie Cadman Richardson and Irene Dunham were most helpful when I visited the Fryeburg Historical Society. I had a delightful conversation with Joan Cowan at the Canaan, Vermont Historical Society when I turned up unexpectedly on a beautiful summer's day. I received a warm welcome from the Friends of Cedar Mountain and the Culpeper Historical Society when I visited the lovely town of Culpeper, Virginia. The librarians and staff at Bowdoin College George Mitchell Special Collections Library and Schlesinger Library at Radcliffe University were always gracious in helping me find the materials needed to build the historical structure beneath the story.

In fact, my biggest thank you has to go to the amazing people who stand as guardians to our past. Those dedicated souls who spend their time discovering and preserving the stories and artifacts that show us where we come from and what we can achieve. During the researching of Phebe's story, I have traveled around Maine, into Vermont, and to the Blue Ridge of Virginia. Every time I walked into a library or a museum and said, "I'm writing a book....," immediately, these guardians started opening file cabinets, vaults, books, and boxes. They willingly shared their time and knowledge with me and put me in touch with others who were "sure to know." I can't count the number of fascinating conversations I had while leaning over fragile letters or stained photographs side by side with a newfound friend. They are the guardians of great treasures and some of the most interesting people I know.

With sincere gratitude,

Caroline Grimm

Lark's Haven
Bridgton, Maine
2013

Wild Sweeps the Wind

Wild sweeps the wind o'er wood and wold
Like reeds the tall trees bend and sway
Round homes where hearth fires bar the cold
In whose red light the children play
Like reinless steeds they hurry past
I weep on nor rest till morning light;
The moaning of a wilder blast
Is echoing through my Soul tonight.

From the diary of Phebe F. Beach

September 12, 1897

Portland, Maine

Mary's face was lined with fatigue. New lines drawn on her young face from long months of nursing her mother. The train ride back from Fryeburg added more exhaustion. The clanking and swaying of the train had brought on another wretched headache. The chill of the cemetery still lay in her bones and the death of her beloved mother weighed her heart down. Opening the door of the apartment she'd shared with her mother during the last few difficult years, Mary entered and wearily set down her reticule. She went to the tiny kitchen and put the kettle on for tea. She looked around the small apartment--such a far cry from the large, sprawling house they once lived in. All that remained of her mother was a few personal belongings. Her clothes, some beloved books, some precious photographs. Such small remainders to show for sixty years of tumultuous living.

The busy sounds of the streets of Portland distracted Mary from her sad thoughts. She stood looking out the bedroom window as carriages passed and people rushed about, busy with the day-to-day frenzy of life. She stood sipping her tea from her mother's favorite cup. How many times she had stood just so during her mother's illness. Sometimes yearning so fiercely to be gone. To be free from the responsibilities thrust too soon upon her shoulders. By turns bitter and sorrowing, so much of her youth had been twisted and gnarled by her mother's pains and moods.

Mary was long since removed from blaming her mother. She had given up on that during her transition into womanhood. She had seen how so many others were impacted by the war, too. She saw empty sleeves that had once housed a strong arm. An empty trouser leg that once held a dancing limb. And she had seen the far-away stares of those who had never truly come home from the battlefields of the South.

The War. Oh, how she hated The War. It had colored her childhood in shades of blue and gray. The ghosts of The War hid behind doors and under beds. She saw it in her mother's eyes, in her father's angry outbursts. In a neighbor's suicide. So many deaths. So many wounded. So many orphans. The shameful waste of it all.

Mary sat her teacup down and looked around the small bedroom she shared with her mother since that morning when they left Fryeburg and Mary's father, never to return. It was a weary business, this living. She stepped over to her mother's armoire and opened the door. She leaned into her mother's clothing to catch the scent of violets. The scent of mother and safety and warmth. She opened a drawer and pulled out a pair of her mother's gloves. The finest workmanship. Left over from her mother's carefree, younger days. She smoothed the gloves with tender fingers and slid them back into the drawer. As she did, she saw the corner of a school composition book. The kind of book she'd learned to write her letters in during her school girl days. Curious, she pulled the book out and glanced at the cover. In her mother's neat writing were the words "The Diary of Phebe F. Beach, Esquire 1857" Mary glanced in the drawer again and saw several more composition books, a bundle of old letters, and an envelope with her own name written on it. She opened the envelope and began to read her mother's words to her.

August 26, 1897
Portland, Maine

My Dear Mary,

I do not know when you will read this letter. I dearly hope it will not be for many years, but I fear the time will come sooner rather than later. There is much I must tell you and so much I still cannot bring myself to tell you to your face.

First, dear girl, I must apologize to you. I fear I have done you a great wrong. My illness has kept you from enjoying your young womanhood. I know you have not married because you would not leave me. For that, I love you more than I can ever express. I wish with all my heart that could have been different. I wanted so much for you. I wanted you to live the life of your own choosing. No mother wants her daughter shackled with cares and burdens as you have been with me.

I know you would say it was your desire to care for me. You have always been a good girl like that. I have tried so to be strong and to overcome the weakness and pain that has me returning to my bed over and over again. I do not know why I must suffer so. Surely, our Heavenly Father must have some purpose in it all.

Mary, dear, I must counsel you as to what you should do when I am gone. You are a young, modern woman and you have many more choices than I had at your age. My wish is that you will choose your own path. One thing you must not do is return to your father's house. Oh, Mary, he does love you so. Do not doubt that. But your poor father has not been the same since the war. He is one of the lost ones. To the outside world, he appears well, but he harbors demons. You well remember his rages. I protected you as much as I could, and I am sorry I could not do more. Without me to protect you, I think you would bear the full force of his troubled mind. Your aunt does what she can with him, and she is able to soothe him where I could not.

I would rather you went to stay with your cousins or took a teaching position than to have you return to Fryeburg. I hope to be able to leave you a little money to tide you over until you can find a suitable position.

Mary, I ask your forgiveness. I have not been the mother I would have liked to be. If I have an excuse for that it would be the sorrows I have known and the loss of so many I held dear. But I will not make excuses. I should have held you closer. I should have tried to be a more loving mother. You knew me only as a task master and then as a frail invalid. That is not how I would have you remember me. I was not always this way.

It is pure vanity on my part, dear, but I wanted you to know me. To know me when I was young and carefree. To know me during those terrible war years when our lives were torn apart. And to know me after the war when we all tried so hard to get on with our lives, to pretend the war never happened. But we were all changed. Our lives could never again be carefree. So many young lives were destroyed, so many tears were shed. We could not move beyond the horrors of those bloody, heart-breaking years.

I fear that is my legacy to you, Mary. We could not help but pass all of our pain down to your generation. Our childhood playmates were shattered on those far away battlefields. Those that returned lived always in the shadow of those days. The women, the parents, the children who stayed at home lived with constant worry and the fear of a letter bringing bad news. Not one of us was untouched by the war. This is the cost of human folly.

My darling girl, how much it meant to me to bring you into this world. To give life when so much of life had been taken. You were the return of all the good we had lost in those terrible years. You brought back my joy. After the horror of those war years, you brought the preciousness of new, innocent life to your father and me. In those early days of your life, your smile was the sunshine that kept the shadows at bay. I thank God for you. So, if you ever wonder if I loved you, my darling, please know that you meant all of creation to me.

Your loving mother,

Phebe F. Page

Mary sat her mother's last letter down on the bed. With tears rolling down her cheeks, she picked up her mother's diary. Opening the cover, she found a second letter written fifteen years before.

January 30, 1880
Fryeburg, Maine

My dear daughter,

I write this letter for you. You are just thirteen and like all thirteen year old girls, you have stars in your eyes and romantic notions of how your life will be. In school, you learn about the war, and you dream of handsome brave soldiers marching off to save the Union. You dream of steady women who yearn for the return of their men while muscling sturdily through the farming chores and knitting stockings for the poor boys in the field. And you dream of the joys of those men returning from battle, tired and worn and sweeping those women off their tired feet, returning them to life as it was before.

I have never told you about those times. It is too soon to speak of them. The wounds of that awful war are still too keen. The losses too painful for words. But I long for you to know me as I was, not as I am. To know me as a young girl with dreams and stars and my whole life before me. Perhaps someday I can speak of those times, but for now, I will write them down and some distant day when I am no more you may read them, and I pray you will understand.

My early days are mysterious to me. I know only what others have told me. As a baby I came to live with my Aunt and Uncle Fessenden in South Bridgton, Maine. They had no children of their own, a grave disappointment that Aunt took especially hard. They made up for their lack of children of their own by taking in the children of others. Uncle's nephew, Will Barrows, lost both his parents in a matter of weeks to a throat distemper epidemic. This tragedy brought Will to live in South Bridgton where he was raised and educated with great love. One of Aunt's nieces, Mary Frizzell, came from Vermont as a baby and lived with them, too. I came soon after I was born, and together we made a family.

Uncle was a Congregational minister, parson of South Bridgton's church. In the pulpit he was a holy, towering power, scaring the youngsters with his warnings of hellfire and eternal damnation. He was an ardent abolitionist and a strong temperance man, preaching often on the evils of slavery and strong drink. To me though, he was just Uncle. Kind, jovial, affectionate. He had bushy eyebrows that I loved to tug as a little child, and there was such kindness in his eyes, such compassion. I adored him.

Aunt was a little woman as all the Beach women are. Short in stature, but long on the observances of propriety. She had lovely auburn hair which she kept sternly pulled back in a tight bun all her days. As a little girl, I most loved those moments as she readied for bed when she undid her hairpins and let her hair fall. She let me brush it out for her with my clumsy little fingers. One hundred strokes a night, she'd say, keeps your hair strong and healthy. To this day, I do the same at night. It soothes me and brings back those memories of a mostly carefree childhood.

I say mostly carefree because of a memory I have. I must have been about three at the time. My parents, Samuel and Sarah Beach, had come to visit me. We sat in the guest parlor with Aunt and Cousin Mary. Mary and I each had a tea biscuit while the grown-ups talked, and we sat quietly as we'd been taught to do. I do not know what the trouble was with the grown-ups, but I remember feeling uncomfortable. As they talked, they kept glancing my way, and I thought I might have committed some transgression although I could not think what it might have been.

After a time, my parents stood up rather abruptly, and Aunt walked them to the door. A child can tell with grown-ups when they are upset and acting polite. Aunt mentioned the blackberry jam she *had put up the day before and went to fetch a jar for them to take with them.*

While Aunt was out of the room, my mother picked me up, and she and my father quickly walked out of the house and climbed into their carriage. My father flicked the reins, and the horse started off down the driveway. As the carriage turned onto the road heading up Barker's Hill, my father urged the horse to a faster pace. I remember laughing with joy at the fast pace and my mother holding me tight against her.

We dashed away up the hill, down the other side, and on towards Sebago. As we headed up the hill at a breakneck pace, the poor horse stumbled and the carriage tipped over. I was thrown clear. I remember that feeling of flying through the air so slowly as though the air was thick like hot taffy. And I remember hitting the ground and the pain of a bump on the head.

My next memory is of Uncle lifting me up and holding me close to his black coat. He smelled of bay rum and horses and safety, and I wept and shook in his arms. I remember my mother crying and my father's angry voice. Uncle kissed my hurt head and turned to hand me to my friend Leander Frost, the village blacksmith. Leander held me in his strong arms and teased me out of my tears with his usual joking. I reached into his shirt pocket where he always kept sweets for his little friends.

Leander walked me away from the others, and I helped him check over the poor horse to be sure her leg was sound. Uncle and my parents were arguing, and I could tell Uncle was very angry because he was using his pulpit voice. At the time, I did not understand what the trouble was, but later I came to find out. My father was a sinner. He was intemperate. Aunt and Uncle wanted my mother to come to South Bridgton and live with us, but she would not leave my father. I was the focus of a fight for custody. In the end it was thought best if I stayed with Aunt and Uncle. My parents were always a part of my life, but my home was with Uncle.

The rest of my childhood was passed with great pleasantness. My cousins, Will and Mary, were brother and sister to me. Will was older, and he spoiled us, calling us pet names and coddling us. He shared his school books with us, and Mary and I both began learning Latin and mathematics at a young age. Uncle believed that girls should get as good an education as boys, and he set us to our lessons early. We grew up with books and scholarly discussions. We learned about world affairs and parish troubles. Every Sunday was devoted to church. It was as fine a childhood as anyone could have. We had plenty of playmates. Besides the local children, we had cousins by the score who came often to stay in the tidy parsonage we called home.

The tidiness of the parsonage was Aunt's doing. She arose before dawn each day, intent on being a good parson's wife. Her greatest challenge was managing the household on a parson's pay. The congregation was made up of mostly farmers and tradesmen, and cash money was hard to come by. Economy was Aunt's best sermon. There is a joke within the family that Aunt received a paper of pins as a wedding gift, and she used those same pins through all her long married life. She was not one to waste. She believed in hard work and righteous living.

Mary and I were trained at a young age to observe the proprieties and to be proper young ladies. There was acceptable behavior and unacceptable behavior. Aunt was quick to point out the difference between the two when we crossed that line. Never cruel, she admonished us gently and firmly to walk the narrow way. Like all young people, the narrow way often chafed us and felt as restrictive as the corsets I would one day be forced to wear. But looking back, I can see why it mattered to be taught right from wrong. If only we, as a nation, had learned that lesson by a kindly hand rather than by the horrors of the battlefield. But that was all in the future.

The village of South Bridgton was idyllic and pastoral. Tree-lined streets and friendly neighbors. My world as a child was made up of home, church, school, and the corner store with regular stops by the blacksmith shop to see my friend, Leander Frost. Just across the way from the parsonage was Adams Pond, the scene of summer swimming and winter ice skating. The store and post office were just up the road with the church and school around the corner.

The store is where everyone gathered during the week. The menfolks stood about discussing politics and the weather and crops. The women talked of homely details of births, sicknesses, marriages, and deaths. Aunt always followed these happenings with great interest, not as a gossip, but as a Christian woman ready to lend a hand to those in need. So often when a woman in "an interesting condition" came to her time of travail, her older children stayed at our house. There always seemed to be room under the eaves of that great house especially for the young ones. I think Aunt filled her need for children by borrowing the children of others as often as possible. It did her much good and provided a blessing to their parents.

I suppose in any age, politics divide, but in the time of which I speak, the whole country seemed frayed by the divisions. There were arguments and sometimes outright fights over differences of opinion. I was too young to fully understand the problems then. They seemed a matter for grown-ups, and my friends and I would roll our eyes and skip off to whisper and giggle about matters of greater importance. I could not know then how much these divisions would change my own life and the lives of so many I loved.

One issue of the day that I did have strong opinions of my own about was slavery. Uncle's opinions on the topic were widely known. Not only did he trumpet them from the pulpit in South Bridgton, but he wrote of them in well-known publications read in all the country. Uncle was an abolitionist through and through. Many an evening was spent en famille with us all sitting in the family parlor with a crackling fire, Aunt at work on darning stockings or some other handwork, Will and Mary and I listening as Uncle read from Mr. Garrison's paper, The Liberator.

Now, the female gender was not supposed to have opinions on such things, but I considered myself to be an abolitionist at an early age. It was proper for us to leave such weighty matters up to the menfolks. This always rankled me. Was I not as much allowed to opinions as a man? I was educated and thoughtful and thought I should be able to speak my mind. Uncle encouraged me so, but Aunt cautioned me and admonished me for it.

As I grew older I saw many ways that a woman was considered to be less than a man, and it troubled me. Women were relegated to a few prescribed roles in life, and I saw this as unfair. We had only a couple of paths open to us. We could teach school. We could get married. Most women who taught school only did so for a short time. Once they married, their life was about home and children. To not marry was seen as a tragedy. What became of a woman with no husband to protect her and support her? She was at the mercy of whatever relative took pity upon her and gave her a home when her parents were gone.

I had no interest in getting married. All marriage did was turn a woman into a stocking darner and a baby manufacturer. Glorious! I wanted something more. I wanted to travel to faraway places. I wanted to be a writer and tell of all I'd seen. I never voiced those desires. I knew better than that. Aunt would have been so disappointed by my wishes. She would have told me in her gentle but firm way that this was a path not open to good Christian girls. Better to accept the everyday pleasures and trials of home and hearth.

I became Uncle's helpmeet with his abolition work. I served as his amanuensis when he wrote his letters. I helped him in other ways, as well. We did not speak of it ever then, but I suppose now it is safe to speak. South Bridgton served as a stop on the Underground Railroad. Our Fessenden relatives in Portland were involved as well. Slaves who got as far as Portland were sent around Sebago Lake on either the west or east side depending on which was deemed safest. Those who came through South Bridgton were usually hidden in my cousin, Jonathan Fessenden's house, in a secret room above the fireplace next to the chimney. This was a hard location to keep secret being as the house sits between the store and the schoolhouse and church. Other than that, its central location was perfect for bringing in the poor, wretched fugitives.

Those slaves needed food and clothing, and often in the evenings as we listened to Uncle read, Aunt and Mary and I would be stitching simple sturdy clothing in anticipation of another "delivery." I never saw this work as a burden. I saw it as a way I could contribute to the end of slavery. We knew first-hand of the danger our involvement brought to us.

Uncle had been threatened by the militia in the neighboring town of Denmark. It was said that if he preached against slavery one more time, the militia would bring a cannon and shoot a cannonball down the aisle of the church. Uncle, with the courage of his convictions, continued to preach against slavery, but cooler heads must have prevailed in Denmark because no cannon appeared.

On another occasion, a mob formed, intent on tarring and feathering Uncle. A most awful thought to have my beloved Uncle helpless as a mob poured boiling tar on him. I was a young child at the time, but I remember the fear, and I remember Aunt's panic and tears as she pled with Uncle to leave with the neighbors who would protect him. Uncle would not leave his home and his family. He met the mob on our front doorstep. He talked to them in reasoned tones, admonishing them as to their Christian duties and charity. The mob dispersed and became neighbors once again, each returning to his own home. How strange it was to see those men about town after that. Uncle always nodded to them, acknowledged them. They would drop their heads or look away, embarrassed, I think, by their hotheaded actions.

Because of the central location of cousin Jonathan's house, there were times when it was not safe for deliveries of fugitive slaves. Cousin Jonathan was a doctor, and sometimes he would be called away from home during the night which made for difficulties for those deliveries as well. At those times, the fugitives were either moved on to the next stop or delivered to an alternate location. Our barn proved a near-perfect secondary drop-off point. When these unexpected guests arrived, Aunt made no fuss or mention of the extra mouths to feed. She simply watered down the stew or opened up some of her store of canned goods. As a young child, I was not allowed to witness these activities because the less we knew, the less likely we'd be to reveal those secrets.

When I was about the same age as you are now, Mary, I was allowed to take food and clothing to the barn with Aunt. There I saw a man with black skin and tired eyes. He was dirty and wearing rags. Through the tears in what was left of his shirt, I could see the whip scars on his back. It frightened me to see what one human being could do to another. And beyond the fear, I felt an emotion I had never experienced before. Rage. I cannot tell how strongly that affected me, but can only say that from that moment on I was as firm an abolitionist as my uncle.

As I grew towards womanhood, my family began changing. Will, who was a number of years older, had gone off to further his studies at Uncle's alma mater, Bowdoin College. He wrote such lonesome letters home to us, missing each of us and our family life together.

My cousin, nay, my sister, Mary took a position as a school teacher and moved away. Although I was exceeding proud of her, I missed her terribly. I took a quilt she made me, rolled it up and tied it with string and called it Beulah Anne Orff. I took Beulah to bed with me at night to keep me from getting too lonesome for Mary. We were so accustomed to being together through all our growing up years. Aunt missed her terribly, too. She wrote so many instructional letters to her about making sure she buttoned up her coat and wore her scarf and behaved properly. Mary and I would laugh about that in our letters to each other.

Then came what was at that point in my life the saddest of all events. My dear sister Mary left us. Always prone to chest infections, she became ill with a troublesome cough. She developed pneumonia, was so very sick. Aunt and I nursed her as tenderly as any patient could be. She lay gasping on her pillow, her hair spread out limp and lank from sweat, her sweet face by turns flushed and pale, her lips cracked with fever, her eyes dull and finally lifeless as her spirit passed from her. She was just twenty seven years old. I'd lost my sister and best friend, and our house was plunged into the deepest mourning.

Of that time, I can still barely speak. Aunt and Uncle's hearts were broken. Will came home for the funeral and wept until his eyes were swollen nearly shut. The neighbors gathered around, supporting us through our grief, bringing food, doing chores, offering comfort. Uncle performed the burial service. I do not know how he got through it without breaking down. We buried my sweet sister in the cemetery by the pond. And we never spoke of that day again. How could we? Even all these years later, even after all the losses that were to come, that loss broke something in me, changed me. Our family was never the same.

When you lose someone dear to you, there is no clear path through the grief. You can only blindly put one foot in front of the other, holding tight to the hand of the Savior who leads us all through the darkest of pathways. And that is what we each did. Grief is such a solitary journey. Each of us must walk that path alone, never knowing if the sun will shine again.

Uncle busied himself with his abolition work and parish matters. Aunt became more brittle, her tone took on a sharpness with Uncle. She was, with me, still kind and firm but never again would we share the closeness she and Mary and I had. And how did I deal with the loss of my sister? I found refuge in the frivolity of being young. I threw myself into the social life of South Bridgton.

In 1857, I was a young woman standing on that fragile threshold between childhood and marriage. One moment I was a carefree girl and at the next I was being encouraged to start thinking of marriage. Marriage was the last thing I wanted in my life. I rebelled against that institution. Marriage was some matter-of-fact existence where I would be forced to live a settled life of one baby after another and endless household chores and never time for laughter. The married couples I knew all treated each other as though there was no love between them, as though their lives together were all about daily chores and feeding the mouths of multitudes of children. That was not a life that I found attractive in the least.

So I began my campaign to keep anything in pants as far away from me as possible. I was not successful in this. They all seemed to flock around me, wanting to walk me home from church, wanting to sit next to me at singing school, wanting to escort me to the fireworks on the 4th of July. They verily were a plague to me.

As fast as I could spurn their attentions through whatever means seemed effective, another would come around making saucer eyes at me and stuttering his way through an invitation. Each time I spurned one, Aunt would lecture me. "Don't be too harsh with Ansel Fitch. He has a good farm, and you'd be close by." "Don't be so quick to send Frank Wiggin away. He feels warmly towards you and would come here to live with us." And on and on.

I could not see why Aunt was so strongly recommending marriage to me when she seemed not to care at all about Uncle beyond washing his shirts and putting his meals on the table. It seemed to me that love, when it comes, does not last beyond the honeymoon. After that, it all becomes very matter-of-fact. If I was to love someone enough to marry him, I would want that love to last beyond the vows. From what I'd seen, though, the love turned stale before the wedding cake.

I say those boys were a plague to me, and that is how I felt at the time. Looking back now, and knowing what happened to those dear young men, I am much ashamed of my behavior towards them. I was carelessly cruel to them. In my youthful pride and foolishness, I could not know how the boys of my young days would sweat and bleed and die to preserve our beloved country. When one is young, life is all about living in the moment and that is what we all did. We thought those carefree days would go on and on. Oh, we knew eventually we would all settle down to work and family, but it was a far distant life, and we were content to be merry and silly.

My friends and I were good girls. Getting in trouble meant we had gone against some social convention. Outwardly repentant, deep down we resented the constraints placed upon us. What harm was there in laughing and flirting with a boy? Or better still, teasing the boys who were smitten with us? We meant no harm. But Aunt in her gentle, chiding way was always there correcting me. I didn't care a fig about any of the young swains who stopped by to ask me to go riding or walking with them. I was young and carefree, and I wanted to enjoy my life and have a fine time. Still I felt I must listen to Aunt and show her the honor, respect, and obedience due to her.

Uncle never chided me about all the boys hanging about the house. Instead he joked with me in his good-natured way. He told me I could stay at home forever and take care of him when he was old. I told him I would do just that since he was the only creature in pants I could abide. Every Sunday, after the morning church service, Uncle would watch with a twinkle in his eye to see which young man was vying for the honor of seeing me home from church. I often managed to escape their attentions by staying close to Uncle. What young man, after hearing Uncle preach against the sins of the flesh, would dare approach the parson's niece while she stood next to him holding his bible? Such a wicked wretch I was and how I laughed about this with my friends.

Mary, I do not know if you can understand the constraints we had upon us as young women. Living in the modern age as you do, perhaps it seems stuffy and old-fashioned. I certainly thought so when I was young. I had dreams of being a writer. I wrote stories and essays for school and for our Lyceum and also my own newspaper. How I would have enjoyed being able to follow my love for writing as a profession. To feel the words flow across the page. To know my voice was heard in the world. To leave something lasting behind. But it was not to be. The war changed all our lives and destroyed our dreams.

My daughter, I do not want you to grieve for my losses. It is too great a burden for you. I bore them as best I could, but I would not wish others to suffer as we all did. And in truth, my life was not all hardships and heartbreak. I remember the laughter, too. The sweet, carefree, lilting laughter before the wild wind swept it all away. If I could but give you that laughter and joy for your own life, it would be the greatest gift I could give.

Your affectionate mother,

Phebe F. Page

Mary lay down upon her mother's bed, feeling closer to her mother than she had in years. She turned on the electric light against the encroaching dusk. Her fingers lovingly traced her mother's handwriting. Turning the pages of her mother's diary, she began to read the words her mother had written so many years before.

Diary of Phebe F. Beach, Esquire

South Bridgton, Maine 1857

June 27, 1857

This is a most beautiful day. My cousins, Nancy and Mary Barrows, are here on a visit. Aunt decided it was a perfect time for jam-making since we had two such able sets of hands with us. We gathered in the kitchen and all worked in the most pleasant harmony with much talk and laughter shared.

They all insisted that I should begin keeping a journal, and Aunt was most insistent. They said it would be most amusing for me to look over when I am old. I was not convinced it was worth the effort. Cousin Nancy remarked something about my fine talent for writing, and the compliments were echoed from all sides, much to Aunt's gratification. I believe she does enjoy hearing me praised. But flattery doesn't make much impression on me, for I know folks don't mean what they say half the time. I verily believe the only reason why they all want me to write a journal is not because I can "write so well" or because it would be so interesting or anything of that sort. I think it is simply because they think I should have much to write about from so many silly, foolish things that I had said or done, that reading them over might make me wiser.

I don't care about any of that though. I am going to keep a journal. Perhaps part, or all of it, will be foolish, but no one will see it but myself! So I've taken my pencil tonight, and this is the first page of the journal of Miss Phebe F. Beach, Esquire, South Bridgton, Maine, June 27, 1857.

June 29, 1857

Well, I can't think of anything very remarkable to inscribe on this page.

I had a lovely walk this afternoon. I returned after sunset and sat down on the doorstep to rest and make a wreath for my cat out of the flowers I had gathered. Mr. Frank Wiggin has been staying with us, and he came and sat down by me. He asked me why I did not tell him I was going to walk. I told him because it was none of his business where I went. Then he got up and walked off. Aunt came to the door and asked me to be a little careful or I should hurt Frank's feelings. (Oh dear, I wish I could hurt them so they would stay hurt for a good fifty years.) His feelings must not have been too hurt because it was not five minutes before he was back again on the doorstep. He wanted to know if I would not like to take a ride the coming fourth of July. I told him that depended on the company I should have on that ride. He said he hoped I would not object to his company. I said I should not object to it so long as it was at a distance. After this sally, he took himself off and did not return.

I wonder if the young folks will get up a ride for The Glorious Fourth. Caroline Fitch was saying something to me about it the other day, and I promised to go! Gracious goodness! I guess I've lost my chance for going now. I rather think my ride is done for. I don't care though. I can fire some crackers when the rest go by. Well never mind.

I want some "grievous disappointment" to chronicle in order to make my journal romantic.

July 1, 1857

I wish some great catastrophe would happen to somebody (not me of course) so that I might have something of importance to set down in my journal. But I suppose every one's journal (who is foolish enough to keep one) is made up of everyday incidents, mixed up with a startling love adventure now and then.

This morning the delectable Mr. Jacob Choate called and invited me to go up on Pleasant Mountain with his honored self, 4th of July. I told him I was "engaged and could not." This was, I am sorry to say, a lie. But it caused him to go off just as nicely as if it had been the truth, and that was all I cared for. (I wonder what I shall think of this performance when I "am old."

This afternoon I went out to work in my flower garden. I was just thinking what Jake would say if the truth ever came out, and he should find that my engagement was to remain quietly at home all day on the fourth. Just as I was thinking about this, Ansel Fitch came and sat down on the grass. After some preliminary remarks, he said he wished that I should go with him up to the Albany Basin as there was a little party going there to celebrate Independence Day. Of course, I immediately assented, for two very good reasons; one was it would plague Frank Wiggin immensely if I went, and the other was it would be an engagement, and Mr. Choate would not know I had told him a story to get rid of him. Then, I went and told Aunt. She was very much pleased and said we should be quite a pretty couple!! She was glad I was going and with such a fine young man. I think she wishes I was sweet on Ansel, but I am most decidedly not!

July 5, 1857

Yesterday was as fine a day as one could wish. We started our ride about six in the morning. Our party consisted of Frank Wiggin and Cal Fitch, Tom Fessenden and Hannah Powers, Palmer Fessenden and Lizzie Parker, and Ansel and I. We took dinner at Albany, tea at Lovell, and arrived home between 12 and 1 o'clock that night. We passed some beautiful rose bushes. The boys stopped their horses and gathered a lot of roses. Ansel gave me some and told me to keep them, to remember that ride. I put them into the horse's bridle and said I guessed I had torn my dress enough to remember that trip, without the roses. When we parted that night Ansel asked me to take Frank and come up and see them soon. I told him if I had got to take Frank, I wished Cally would meet me half-way, for I thought since Frank had begun to cultivate a moustache, he must be pretty heavy, and I should be tired before I got here. Ansel laughed and said he should tell Frank that. I hope he will.

On the whole, we had quite a good time--enough to eat and plenty of fun.

Aunt inquired all about the excursion and seemed quite interested and pleased with my account thereof.

My dear old uncle plagues me a little about the boys now and then, but says he guesses I never shall get married but shall take care of him when he is old. I tell him I never saw the man yet that I should want for my husband, and I certainly never did.

July 31, 1857

My birthday. I am 20 today!! I ought to put down a sort of a soliloquy in memory of this day, but I don't know how to soliloquize very well. Perhaps I ought to learn how to reflect and moralize more. If anything can make anyone thoughtful it should be the rapid passing away of one birthday after another. And the thought that we have one year less to live. Sometimes I wish I could be more serious and sober, but before I think of it I am just as wild as ever.

Folks have said to me many a time "how can you be so happy all the whole time?" Or "I wish I could be as cheerful always as you are." I don't know what makes me happy, only that I was made so.

It doesn't seem now as if I ever should be sobered down--but time works wonders, I am told.

I must not keep account of every day sayings and doings, or I shall fill my book up too quick.

Next week, I'm going to Fryeburg on a visit, and I guess I'll let my journal rest for the present. Frank is going off, too. Uncle and Aunt will be all alone for a while.

October 24, 1857

I returned from Fryeburg a little more than a week ago. I enjoyed my visit very much. I went to Mr. John Kilborn's yesterday to a sing. It was a most delightful time with more laughing than singing, I think.

I saw the stage stop here a few days ago as I was calling at one of the neighbors and found on my return home that it left Mr. Wiggin, who has made arrangements to board here and attend school for the next two or three months. Frank has commenced courting Cal Fitch with great fury, so I think he will not bother me much. He was up at the Fitch's farm and "sat up" with her last night. Aunt does not seem to fancy Frank's lady. I think she would prefer he were sitting up with me instead. I do not. I hope Frank and Cal will stick tight and long and firm and strong.

October 30, 1857

Ansel was here and spent the evening a night or two ago. I wonder if Frank told him to come. Anyway, he didn't get the chance to "sit up' unless he sat up with Aunt. I was abed before eight.

November 10, 1857

Uncle and Aunt have talked with me quite a time today about getting married! Now that I am the grand old age of twenty, they say it is about time for me to begin to think about the subject at least. Aunt informed me that Frank had talked confidentially with her and wished to know if she thought there was any reason for him to hope for favor in my eyes, or something to that effect. I told her there was no reason for him to hope for any such thing as favor, although I had nothing against Frank as a friend. As a husband, I should hate him soul and body - boots, trousers, and all. Uncle laughed, and Aunt said I might go farther and fare worse. I said I would prefer to go farther anyway and as to faring worse, I didn't think that was possible, and so the subject ended.

November 24, 1857

Uncle preached a very good sermon today, I would write off an abstract of it if I did not think it would be out of place among the nonsense with which I suppose this book will be filled.

Aunt asked me tonight when she was changing her dress if I would be willing to marry Ansel and have him come here to live and take care of her and Uncle. She said she could not help noticing how handsome and intelligent he looked today, and she thought he was a little partial coming home from meeting. I told her if she was so anxious to get me off her hands, I would pick up somebody, but would rather have Jacob than Ansel. Ansel is so Fitchy. She said she was not in any hurry herself. She would like to have me make it my home here always, but if I calculated ever to marry she would advise me not to treat with too much lightness all the chances I had.

I guess the right one has not come along yet, I do.

November 30, 1857

I have to chronicle today the forming of our own literary club, the South Bridgton Lyceum! How much fun we have had concerning it. The few meetings which we have had have been quite interesting. We each write a piece or poem to be collected and published in our paper. Then, each piece is discussed and criticized. The disputants are "on hand" and full of the matter, and the paper is lively and well sustained. And when going home time comes, we have lots of fun.

The second night we met, I got Cal Fitch's beau, the esteemed Mr. Wiggin, away from her and then ran off and left him waiting for me. Last night, Ansel tried his luck but I escaped to Jacob and took refuge in the shadow of that ancient patriarch leaving Mr. Squire Fitch madder than a--I won't say what. I shan't be troubled with him any more, I'll warrant. Next Friday, I must wait on some girl to walk me home, or Jake will be offering his services again. What a plague boys are! I hate the sight of a coat and breeches anywhere and everywhere.

Frank seems to be rather soft lately. I know Elder Wiggins is a fine young man, as ever lived for fame or glory. But he has one failing, and it is this. He's a little weak in the upper story. Oh, Frank! Your brains ain't as strong as they might be, or you wouldn't have acted so like a sick gander the other night when you said over that mess of stuff and offered me your picture. Beautiful copy of the Sublime Original!!!! I can remember you, Sir, nose and all, without your likeness or even a lock of your greasy old wig to remind me of your existence! I guess I must write a piece of poetry on you and your hopes for the "Student's Offering" at the Lyceum. You seem to be quite inconsolable to think your efforts meet with no better success. Aunt says you are losing your appetite! Verily, your woes should be in print! What shall be the title of my article concerning your prospects, Brother Wiggins? I guess I'll call it "Love's First Young Smash Up." That's it! Now if your ears don't burn next Lyceum night especially, I shan't be to blame.

December 10, 1857

I have had quite a time since I last wrote in my journal. Ansel got mad because I came home with Jake. And having found out by some means, which was my piece in the last paper. He satisfied his animosity by criticizing my poetry to death and destruction. I suppose he thought I should never get over feeling bad to think he, of all others, had found fault with me. Verily, I don't see how I have survived till the present moment!!

But the fun of it was, after he had finished reading his criticism, he sat looking at me as hard as possible to see what impression he had made, I suppose. I turned to the girl who sat next me and began to ridicule and make sport of his criticism till every girl on the seat was stuffing her handkerchief into her mouth to keep from laughing out loud, and Ansel's face was redder than the rising sun.

After we got home, I took to fooling. I declared I should not be able to sit up the next day as my feelings were in such a condition after that criticism. And if I was able to leave the house within a fortnight it was more than could be reasonably expected! I continued my great melodrama until Frank seized the candle and said he was so lame laughing that if he stayed any longer, he never should be able to get up stairs to bed.

After he had gone, I started to go to my room. Aunt took my hand as I was passing her and said, "Don't carry this too far, Phebe. Remember, the Fitches are well set with a good, successful farm. Ansel is a good fellow and don't make him really provoked. He thinks a good deal of you."

I answered I guessed he would think considerable more of me before he was done with it. If he or anyone else thought I cared one copper what he thought of me, they were vastly mistaken. And then I went to bed.

Do you suppose I'd ever have anything to say to that sputtering, huffy, jealous, pated imp of deformity! No sir, by the "Howly St. Pether." Not I. Only I'll take him "down a peg or two" in the next paper and let him see how he likes it? I don't care if the Fitches are "set." What's that to me? I hope he will "set" till he hatches.

December 12, 1857

Frank told me last night that he asked Ansel if he knew that piece he criticized so hard was mine. Ansel said yes, and he did it to see if I cared anything about what he said or thought. And Frank said Ansel asked him if he thought I did care for his opinion. Ansel wanted to know of me whether I didn't care for him or did. Isn't that smart!!!!

I told Frank he needn't trouble himself to tell Ansel anything, I would let him know how much I thought of him before long. I don't care for third parties in my affairs.

December 25, 1857 Christmas Day

Ansel called the other evening and asked me to ride. I inquired very coolly whether Frank told him to. His temper began to rise, and he asked what in the world I meant. I told him, "Oh, nothing, only I didn't know but Frank might have suggested it, as a good way for you to ascertain whether I was vexed or not at the sweet disposition you showed in criticizing my piece." And I offered to tell him all about that without his taking the trouble to carry me to ride. He said he was sure he didn't know he had been treading on anybody's toes. If he had have known it was my piece he would have done differently. I told him he need not make any excuses. I thought I should live through it all. I told him I was altogether too much used up to go to ride, and I thought he better not venture forth, without a thicker hat, or he would take cold in his brains. He had been using them so much lately, they might be more easily afflicted by exposure. The gentleman then arose and left very abruptly without even wishing me good evening. The saucy dog!

January 25, 1858

All things go on about so. Nothing new or interesting has transpired of late. Lyceum still continues. The paper has been the cause of some little trouble among the more sensitive members of the Lyceum. Several who have been attacked, have come to me to help them write a piece in retaliation. I don't know as it is worthwhile to spend one's time fighting even on paper, but I'll help those who are imposed on and haven't wit enough to help themselves. And then, I can fight my own battles.

Cal put in a piece about "woman's wit being quick to revenge a real or fancied slight," in which she endeavored to hit everybody in general, me in particular. So I concluded it was best to give her a "return flash" entitled "Courting Gals," in which I dwelt at some length on girls who did their own courting and then attempted to assist their brothers and sisters in theirs. The piece was received with "tremendous applause!" I caused considerable merriment. Cal did not know it was me that wrote it, and she set about scolding two or three. Then, finding she had got hold of the wrong ones, laid it to me. She did not say much, but she hasn't ever looked at me since she found out I was the Author. Which on the whole is rather awful!! Not at all, not at all!

May Perley and I entered into agreement to wait on each other home every night so we have done so every night but one. Then May stayed with Diana Hall and so went home another way. As I was in the entry getting my bonnet, Albert Burnham, Esquire proposed to "see me home." I excused myself and soon after, as I was going out the door, Colonel Perley stopped me to speak with me. As we were talking, Albert passed with another girl on his arm. He waited in the dark yard till I came along and then offered me his other arm. I was confident he thought I was another person so I joined. I knew the girl he had on his other arm was going in an opposite direction from what I was, and some way too. I wanted to see how he would manage. After he found out who I was, I never saw such a piece of work in my life as he made with his spluttering and excusing. Finally, when I had tormented him long enough, I told him I thought I was walking some distance to accommodate him and as I didn't care about going more than a mile out of my way, even for the sake of having his company, I guessed I would go home. So I left him.

Mr. Staples, the high school teacher, got hold of the story and told Frank, so Frank asked Albert about it, and Albert told him he wouldn't go through that again for any sum of money. He said if the earth had only opened up and swallowed him that night he would have thanked the Lord. How I do love to plague everybody. That scrape has made fun enough for us all to last a month. Albert has called twice on purpose, he said, to see me about that "unfortunate affair," but I managed to be engaged both times and told Frank to tell him I could not see him, he must call again. I wonder how many times he will call.

February 20, 1858

School is done. Lyceum is closed. Frank has departed to visit some of his friends, and if I was ever lonesome I might be now. But not long, for my cousins, Sam, Susy, and Martha Bradley, are coming from Fryeburg this week or next.

William Fessenden has been here for several days. He has been sick. And he likes me too well--so I haven't seen him much. Aunt thinks the world of him. Somehow, he doesn't suit me though, and I am glad he is going soon. Aunt might be wanting to make a match for me, if he wasn't any relation - as it is, that game is up even though he is not a blood relation.

March 1, 1858

Sam and Sue and Martha are here. Thankfully, W.F. has gone. One evening not long before he went, we were alone in the room, and he tried to kiss me. Of course, I wouldn't allow him more than a cousin's kiss, and I was just contrary enough not to let him do even that. I kept him at a distance by playing the fool with him awhile when all of a sudden he asked me not to "fool" for a little while. I told him he was the fool, and an impertinent wretch to call his cousin sappy names. He wanted to know how many more times I was going to remind him he was my cousin. I said till I thought he could remember it. He said he did remember it, and putting his arm around me, he commenced saying something sappy. I knew the time had come, and springing up I told him my cat was squalling, and I must go and let him in. So I left and as it took me some time to find my cat and let him in, I did not get back into that room, that night.

If anybody should attempt to make love to me, I'm afraid I couldn't help laughing right in their faces. I suppose I don't do right. I should be more serious, but somehow I can't.

I didn't see W.F. alone again till he went away. We parted very good cousins, and W.F. said he should write to me. Aunt acts (and has for some time) as if something didn't suit her, I don't know what it is, and I don't care. It can't be that she thinks one who is all but a cousin ought to be any more nearly related. If she does, I don't, and there's the end of it. Besides, if he wasn't my cousin, I wouldn't want him if he got a thousand dollars a year! Oh, but boys are a plague to me!

March 10, 1858

An exciting happening in my life! I got a letter the other night from Cousin Nancy's husband, Mr. Yeaton, the Principal of a high school in New Gloucester. He offered me a job at the town school in their district to teach the ensuing summer. Wages are $5.00 per week. He wishes me to board in his family and teach his pupils drawing and writing. I think I shall go. Aunt favors the idea and so does Uncle, though they are afraid it will be too hard for me. I don't think so and shall write that I will accept. School commences the first week in May.

March 27, 1858

I have been very busy lately, and shall be so for some time to come, getting ready for my summer's work. I have written that I will take the job at the school. Cousin Sam Bradley has gone to Canada to get a situation as engineer or something of the sort. Cousin Joe Frizelle has written me quite an entertaining letter of his travels. Our household is in a flurry as I prepare for my departure.

April 4, 1858

There is plenty of sewing still on hand, and numberless visits to neighbors waiting to be endured. I shall get the sewing all done in season. I don't know about the visits. Martha and Sue are here and want me to make some visits with them as they are not much acquainted in the neighborhood. Aunt says I ought to go around some with my cousins, so I think I may make some visits though I do not have the time.

April 27, 1858

It has been some time since I have written in my journal. Frank is here on a visit. He wanted to know how I am going to New Gloucester. He says he is going to Lewiston to school about the same time I go. I know he would like to accompany me, for Lewiston is very near New Gloucester. I'll put Sue up to making him propose it. Then that will plague Cal Fitch more than a little, and we are bound to pay her back for a few little things, Sue and Martha and I. It will help to even the score.

April 30, 1858

Frank has proposed accompanying me to New Gloucester, and he has been accepted! He inquired in a very deferential manner whether it would not be agreeable to me to have some one on my journey to look out for my baggage, etc. He said it would give him the greatest pleasure to accompany me as far as he was able to. Well, I expressed eternal and everlasting felicity at the very idea of the proximity of his invaluable self during my travels, and so it is arranged that we leave for foreign parts next Saturday. Then we shall arrive at our destination the same day and be in readiness to commence our schools the ensuing Monday. Sic Tempus Fugit-Hurrah Boys! Clear the track for Wiggin, Beach and Co.!

New Gloucester 1858

May 20, 1858

I guess my journal won't get much attention unless I have more time than I have had since I've been here, to write in it. I commenced school on Monday. I had over fifty scholars, some of them older and larger than myself. I was examined by the school committee Monday night. We got along very well until we came to a word a committee member asked me to parse. Here we began to quarrel and kept it up some time. I stuck to it, my way was right, and he was confident he was correct. Finally after laboring hard enough to earn a month's additional pay, I succeeded in showing him his errors, and he very gruffly said he "guessed I would answer" and proceeded to write me a teaching certificate forthwith.

I have got along nicely with my school which now numbers over 60. There are ten girls and two young men boarding at Mr. Yeaton's with me. We have nice times singing and playing and drawing and going to walk Saturday afternoons. Eunice Dyer from Portland rooms with me and shares a bed with me, and Belle Miller from Canada occupies another bed in the same room. We have fine times frolicking and fooling. Cousin Nancy says the girls all follow me into any mischief just like a flock of sheep.

May 27, 1858

One of the committee men was in to school a few days ago. He was absent from the place part of the first week and so did not visit me till lately. He spoke very well of my school and told Mr. Yeaton he "considered me a very smart teacher!" Don't I feel considerable smart laboring under such a compliment as that!

Some of my boys are ugly enough to try a saint, to say nothing of a sinner like myself. I kept one the other day until dark to make him behave (if possible). He got every word of his lesson long before dark but as he was going out, after he had recited, he shook his fist at me, when he thought I didn't see him. So I called him back, and told him if he was as fond of me as all that, we would enjoy each other's company a little longer. I kept him till I was nearly starved myself and guess he was. Then, with a few wise admonitions, I allowed him to depart. The next morning he brought me a great bunch of flowers and said he "did like me." The little imp! I almost wanted to kiss him! But I only told him to go along and behave himself then. I don't like keeping school very well anyway.

I have had lots of letters lately--two from Frank. He says he thinks he shall come to New Gloucester and visit my school some Wednesday or Saturday. I guess he won't! I shall write him that I don't keep school on Wednesdays or Saturdays. And in fact, I always dismiss school when company comes. I don't want him visiting me or my school.

June 12, 1858

Last Sunday after meeting, in the afternoon, Louis Haskell told Emma Loring and I, as we were sitting on the doorsteps reading, that they were going to have a sing at a nearby house that afternoon, and we must come and tell the rest of the young ladies to come. So we went in and told the girls, and they asked leave of Cousin Nancy to go, and got it, and we all started for the sing. It was not far from five o'clock. We found quite a number of young folks there but after singing two or three tunes, I thought it seemed more like a regular kissing party than a Sunday social sing.

I looked on for a little while and then got up and left the room. I went up stairs after my hat and as I was coming down I met Sam Haskell (Louis' older brother) hunting for me. He snatched my hat and exclaimed "You are not going home, Miss Beach." "Yes sir," said I and held on to my hat. "But look here," said he, "What makes you so sober tonight? You wasn't so when we were at your cousin's the other evening." "No," said I, "Twasn't Sunday then." He looked at me half laughing and said, "I did not know you were a preacher." "I am not," said I, "And never expect to be, but still I hope I have some respect for the Sabbath." He looked down and commenced an apology for speaking as he did. Then the door opened and Emma Loring and Netty Purington came out. They asked if I was going home. I said yes and told them to get their hats and come, too. Emma hesitated a moment. I went toward the door and then stopped and said "Better not think till after you have done it, Em." She laughed and said "Wait for me, then," and ran after her hat and in a moment Netty followed. They came right down, and we all started for home. Sam walked part way with us and then returned to the sing.

Mr. Yeaton was walking in the front yard when we came up to the house. He looked surprised to see us back so soon but said nothing. We went up stairs to our rooms and soon saw him going down towards Mr. Haskell's. It was not very long before we beheld in the distance all the girls with Mr. Yeaton walking behind them coming towards home. They came up and told us, he (Mr. Yeaton) walked down by the house and they supposed he heard something of a noise. Anyway, he called and wished "the young ladies that belongs to his school to accompany him home," he said. Some of them were crying and some scolding. For they said he talked pretty hard to them for not leaving when we did. I don't know as we deserved any more credit for leaving than the rest did for staying, though for we both followed our own inclinations. When I "am old" and read this, perhaps I shall think folks always ought to have right inclinations.

June 17, 1858

After I had dismissed school yesterday, I stood on the dining room stairs looking at some paper animals Franky Yeaton had been cutting out, when James Brackett came in with the letters. All the girls crowded 'round and after he had plagued them a little and disappointed them a good deal, he handed me three. One was from Nell Fessenden, one from Frank, and one from Joe Frizelle. Frank's I tore into three or four pieces without opening it and threw it among the girls. While they were scrabbling for the pieces and trying to fit them together, I sat down and read my two others.

Nelly wanted I should call at her Aunt Keith's and do an errand for her. She wrote she wanted me to become acquainted with her cousins, Lydia Keith and the boys. Phillip is an old "Batch" over thirty somewhat. Lydia is about 30 and Albion younger, "none of them married or engaged," she writes. Now I guess I'll court up that Old Bachelor, that's what I thought when I read the letter. So last night I started, and went up to call on Lydia. I met with a very cordial welcome. I told Lydia I had heard from Nell and did the errand she requested me to with Mrs. Keith. I had a very pleasant call and when I came to go home a little after nine, my friend the old Batch got his hat and very politely waited on me home.

And when we got there, shocking to relate! He kissed me! I was thunderstruck! I did not think of progressing like that the first night of my courtship! But I thought best not to get excited over it, so I only remarked that I thought he was rather *fast* for a gentleman of his *years*. He said 'twas so seldom he got a chance to wait on a real likely girl, he thought he must make an impression somehow. Then he asked if I couldn't give him a kiss to remember me by. By that time I had got my breath, and I told him no I wouldn't kiss him till I got a chance to scare him as bad doing it, as he did me. Then I ran into the house and cousin Nancy asked me who I'd got for a beau. I told her a certain wise old demagogue--Phillip whose surname was Keith, a dweller in that land and one of her kindred. She laughed heartily and said she never heard of his waiting on a girl before, since she lived in New Gloucester. She guessed he must mean something. I said I rather thought he did mean to show me the way home. Then in a day or two, the girls got to talking about "Phillip and Phebe," and so it went.

June 28, 1858

One of the committee undertook to lecture me yesterday about letting my scholars play ball at recess. He is a regular fault-finder and had gotten two or three school mistresses turned away, so they say, for just about nothing. I'd like to have him try to play that game with me. I guess he'd get into something of a scrape.

Tonight after school Phill took me to ride. Verily, my Old Batch is rather more docile than such animals usually are. I had quite a good time. We are beginning to plan for the Fourth of July. Some of the girls go home, some go away to celebrations, and some stay here. Phill asked me tonight if I didn't want to go into Portland and see them celebrate the Fourth. I did not give him a direct answer, though he rather urged it. He said, "We would go to General Fessenden's and see Nell and the rest and have a 'tip top' time."

I would like to see Nelly very much but guess I shall tell him I can't go. I'm afraid the foolish old monkey twister will begin to court in good earnest, and I couldn't go that no how. He's a *leetle* too near his second childhood. I don't want a man quite 15 years older than I am because he would get decrepit and infirm et cetera and so on. And then I should flirt with the young men and then he would be jealous and then he'd storm and then I should scold and then we should fight and then he would sue for a divorce and then he would get it, if I could help him to it, and then we should part and then I should have all the fuss and trouble of being courted again and I should get rather sick at the stomach and have the dyspepsia and probably never see another well day and thus my illustrious life would come to an ignominious end and all on account of marrying my grandfather! *"An ounce of prevention is worth a pound of cure." (Genesis 8:20)* So I guess I'll not go to Portland. No knowing what it may lead to. 'Tis almost eleven, and I must retire. Good night, Old Journal.

July 10, 1858

The Fourth of July has passed. I did not go to Portland and the Gentleman went alone. Netty Purington and I got a carryall and horses and took Lydia Keith and another girl and went for 8 miles to visit a Shaker community. We had a real nice time. We went to see a new building they are just finishing made to accommodate over 40 families. 'Tis very large, and we got rather tired going all over it.

One "good looking" young Shaker went with us to show us around. Just after we left for home, we came to a good watering place and as the horses had not been out of the harness since we started, I thought they must be thirsty. I stopped them and the red one held his head very still for me to unfasten the check rein, but when I came to let down the grey one's head, he was so anxious to get at the water that he kept his head moving so it took me some time to manage him. Just as I got him to drinking, I happened to look 'round and saw the "good looking" young Shaker coming towards us. He said he would water the horses for me. He stopped some time and talked with us. When he was with the other Shakers he was very solemn and said "thee and thou" and spoke but little. When he was with us, he was full of fun and forgot his "thees and thous" entirely. Pretty soon we rode on, and Lydia said she guessed I'd spoiled all that fellow's Shakerism by the way he looked after the carriage. I told her I guessed they had all done their part towards flirting with him, and if he was excommunicated they would just have to help me support him.

We had a splendid ride home. Stopped a little while at Mrs. Keith's and then took our horses to the stable, paid for them, and so ended the Fourth, the "Glorious Fourth of 1858."

July 17, 1858

Phillip had been down and called at Mr. Yeaton's, the first time he ever called there, Cousin Nancy said. The other night he asked me to go to walk. I made some excuse, but after supper it was so pleasant I thought I would go half or three quarters of a mile and call on one of my scholars. So I started. As I passed the store, Phill came out and walked along by me and asked if I had repented saying I wouldn't go to walk. I told him I didn't say I wouldn't go to walk. I only said I wouldn't go with him. Well he said if that was the case, the only thing to be done was for him to go with me. So on he went.

After we had gone a little way I made believe I was tired and wanted to go back. He said we had not gone any way at all yet. So we went on. When we were coming back, I suppose he thought it was time to grow sentimental. So he did his best, but the answers he got were some of them not very romantic or satisfactory. Finally when I said I should be ever so glad when my school was done and

I was free again, he grew indescribably affectionate and endeavored to clasp me devoutly to his heart. I inhumanly frustrated his design by chasing off after a lightening bug that I fortunately saw glimmering under a bush.

When the old gentleman succeeded in overtaking me, he appeared quite composed, and after a few commonplace remarks, he tenderly inquired if there was any particular attraction in Bridgton that made me so glad school was going to finish so soon and I was going back there. "Was there anyone I should be particularly glad to meet, or who was impatient to see me?" "Oh yes," I told him, "Half a dozen or more, just ready to spread their wings and fly away, they were so impatient for my arrival. And I was mightily afraid if I did not get there pretty soon, they would all be gone." He looked at me kind of puzzled and asked if I was ever sober. I demurely told him "I did not know. But anyway, I never was drunk."

He seemed to be satisfied with that declaration. After that, I had gave him to understand that I expected to be married the coming fall and would tell him the name of my intended, only I had unfortunately forgotten it. We parted without one kiss, and he bid me good evening, in a sort of a bewildered frame of mind either as if he was pretty sleepy or just about waking up and went his way.

Yesterday, the girls were making some bouquets of roses and other flowers for some young gentlemen, and Netty made a beauty for Phill's brother, Albion. Nothing would do but I must send Phillip one. So I made one. And a magnificent bouquet it was. The principle "ingredients" were thistles, catnip, potato tops, a small green pumpkin and an "herb" of a sweet smelling savor, the perfume of which somewhat resembled a green tomato vine, some spirits turpentine, and a skunk mixed together. I know it will greatly refresh his smellers. And with this floral offering, I trust my fourth love scrape will close for I verily begin to think I am a fool. And if I am not careful I don't know but somebody else will find it out besides myself.

July 20, 1858

Since last writing in this affair, quite a change has come "over the spirit of my dream." Last Tuesday, that old committee man came into school in the forenoon. At recess, he came and sat down by me and desired me to make some change in my manner of teaching that I did not think was necessary. I told him so, and I said the scholars are getting on well and had been. They were orderly and diligent, as he had seen, and I saw no case in making the change he spoke of, especially as school had but about four weeks longer to keep. Upon this, he got quite vexed and insisted I should do just as he said and hinted that if I did not follow his directions another teacher could be got who would.

I knew by the manner in which he talked that he cared much more about having his own way in the matter than he did for the good of the school. So I made up my mind in two minutes what to do. I knew he threatened about another teacher just to scare me into doing as he said. But I wasn't a bit frightened, wonderful to relate. And just before I dismissed school at noon I remarked that I hoped all would try and be present in the afternoon as school would finish that night. Oh, Moses and Aaron and Peter and Paul!! Didn't Mr. Committee look rather astonished!! He came up to the desk and began to palaver and say how difficult it would be to obtain a teacher for only four weeks! I told him he had mentioned one could be got, and he was at liberty to bring her along as soon as he chose.

Then I took my hat and went out. He followed and observed that he hoped I would think better of my decision to let things go on as they had done.

That night I dismissed for good as I had said. The next day, both committee men called at Mr. Yeaton's, and the fussy one urged my keeping the school the remaining four weeks. The other one merely said he had no fault to find with the school. His children did well and loved the teacher. He was sorry at the state of affairs, but if I declined to continue as teacher, then the gentleman who was the cause of my leaving the school must furnish another mistress. This was just what I wanted, and a fine long job I hope he will have before he gets one to his satisfaction. Mrs. Yeaton said she guessed I was a match for him, but I must stay and continue to teach drawing and painting and writing for her scholars till her school closed which would be in about a fortnight so I have concluded to stop that time here. Then I shall see what success Mr. Gross meets with in getting a new teacher. Folks say he is rather displeased with me. I trust he is.

August 15, 1858

School has closed, and day after tomorrow I leave these parts. Mr. Yeaton goes into Portland, and I go with him, to spend one or two days with Nelly at General Fessenden's, and then I go up to South Bridgton. I shall like to see old Bridgton and some few of its inhabitants after four months absence.

August 20, 1858

Portland

Here I am safe and sound. I am having a very pleasant visit but got a letter from home last night that Uncle was going to Brunswick to a Semicentennial celebration at Bowdoin and as Aunt had thought some of accompanying him. They wanted me to come home as soon as I could, to keep house. So I start tomorrow morning.

August 27, 1858

I have arrived safely at home and found all well. Susy has gone to Fryeburg to attend school this fall and my cousin, Ellen Beach, is here on a visit. Aunt, after considerable hesitation, finally thought she wouldn't go to Brunswick, and so Uncle started last Monday without her. I have not been out much since I returned home. Aunt says nobody can think how long this summer has seemed to her and Uncle without me buzzing 'round. Well it has not seemed very long to me as is the first one I ever spent away from home. Still I am glad to get home and see all the folks in general and my cat, in particular.

I thought that when I got back to Bridgton I would be very dignified and reserved to show the inhabitants of this renowned place that I was something considerable. But I hadn't been here four days before I forgot all about any dignity and cut up a shine that would have done credit to any wild gypsy under the light of the sun. The other night I was coming down street from the post office when Mr. Frost put his head out of the shop window and wanted to know if "his girl" wasn't going to speak to him. Now Mr. Frost was always having over nonsense with me, and he called me his girl and was always ready to do anything for me ever since I was a little young one. So I went up to the window and shook hands with him, and when I saw there was no one around, I talked and laughed with him some time.

Finally, I thought I heard somebody laugh in the shop. "Well now," said I, "Just take your head out of that window and let me see who you have in there. I thought you was all alone." "No, no" said he. "There's somebody in here, but I shan't take my head out of the way. If you want to see who it is, just come in and see. 'Twont be the first time a lady ever was in my shop" "I won't do it," said I, "Until I find out whether he is good looking enough to pay for all that trouble." Mr. Frost looked 'round at somebody I couldn't see and laughed and said "There, Phebe, he's hiding, I declare." "Well," said I, "He's worth finding then, I guess. For if he was some young men or some *rather old ones*, he would be sticking his head out of the window every time a girl went by." I heard somebody laugh again and went 'round into the shop to see if it was anyone I knew. I could not see anybody, but I thought Mr. Frost looked rather knowingly into a certain corner, so I commenced climbing over some old iron in that direction, and my movements disturbed the meditations of a certain individual who flew about in a most surprising manner with my honorable majesty after him.

At length, the gentleman found himself in a place where he could neither climb over nor back out, confronted by a lovely looking damsel in a pink muslin dress and a hat trimmed with green ribbon. I know we must have looked funny, and I guess it was hard telling which was the smuttiest. We were all laughing as hard as we could, and it was sometime before Mr. Frost subsided sufficiently to introduce us as Mr. Jordan, his nephew, and Miss Beach. We shook hands, and I apologized in the most polite manner I could assume for my unmannerly conduct, and he excused himself for his awkwardness in receiving company. And then I left, and Mr. Frost and the gentleman went up to the house.

September 9, 1858

Last Saturday Aunt got a letter from Uncle saying that he was quite sick, and they wanted her to come down to Brunswick and stay with him till he was able to come home. She immediately made preparations to go, leaving Cousin Ellen and I to keep house. She engaged Frank who was stopping at Colonel Perley's to come and stay here nights and milk and take care of the horse and cow, etc. etc. I believe I said something rather unproper when I heard of this arrangement but on the whole I don't care, for everyone knows Mr. Frank is courting Cal Fitch.

We get along very well, only I have a little trouble getting Frank to go a' courting as often as he should to keep appearances in the way I want them kept up. The other night Frank did not come back as usual, it got to be nine o'clock and still he did not arrive. I thought probably he had forgotten his cow and all sublimary matters and had gone to sit up with Cal. I went up to get Nahum Knapp to come and milk but Nahum was gone, so Aunt Nahum said, and they had to get Bill Fessenden to do their milking. So I started to return home. On the way I met Mr. Frost. He asked me to go back to his house and give him a call. I told him it was too late. Frank had given me the mitten, and I guessed on the whole he had better go down and milk our cow. "Well," he said , "he guessed on the whole he would be very glad to, if she hadn't been milked." Somebody just behind me said he "guessed on the whole" Mr. Frost better stay where he was" I looked 'round and saw Mr. Jordan just coming up the road. Then he asked if he wouldn't do as well as Mr. Frost. I told him, "Oh, yes. Better. Because *your* wife wouldn't mind it so much as *some* folk's wife might." Mr. Frost declared I was bound to hit him somehow, and he had a good mind to go now but "on the whole" he concluded not to.

Mr. J. milked and then we all sat down on the doorstep, and Nell was going on about Cyrus Warren. Then who should walk up but brother Wiggin looking rather fatigued and dejected "Well, well" said I, "I thought you had forgotten all about us forlorn maidens and had gone to seek consolation from all earthly woes and trials up to "Mother Fitch's." "Never mind us," said Nelly, "But I guess that cow's bag aches by this time." Frank started for the milk pail glad to escape from our tongues, I know. He walked honestly to the barn and after trying half an hour or so unsuccessfully to get a drop of milk, he called out and wanted to know what "the old harry" we had been doing to that cow to make her hold up her milk so. I asked him, "what the deuce" he meant by swearing. Nelly went to the milking bars and kept encouraging him to try harder.

Finally, Frank threw his milk pail at her and jumping over the boards gave chase. Nelly fled precipitatedly into the house, unceremoniously passing over Mr. Jordan and myself in her haste. Frank was rushing after with an amount of speed I never dreamed he possessed, when his flight was suddenly arrested by some slight impediment which I placed in his way. He stopped in about as much of a hurry as he started. Then he then turned upon me. Mr. J. took my part, and Nelly came back to my rescue so three to one we soon put Brother Wiggin to rout and caused him to beg for mercy. As it was somewhat late by that time, we concluded to adjourn.

September 12, 1858

We get along finely keeping house. Frank says I make splendid custard pies, but he doesn't fancy my eggshell cakes so well. I told him I saw no sense in wasting the shell as it added a fine texture. Cyrus has been here and spent the evening, and Mr. Jordan came down the same night. We had fun enough. Frank had to take it from all sides, for whatever Nelly said Cyrus confirmed and enlarged on, and when they failed to plague him, Mr. J. and I came down upon him like a "thousand of brick". I guess the whole Fitch tribe had their "ears burn" that night. Frank bore it like a martyr. But when I went out into the kitchen to get some water he followed me out and placing his arm around my waist and fixing his big round optics upon me with a sort of die-away expression, he said it hurt his feelings to be plagued about the wrong one, etc. and so forth. Whereupon I sent a dipper full of water down his shirt "buzzum" and asked him if he was going to faint. He came to very speedily and declared I had spoiled his dickey, and he should have a kiss to pay for it. I screeched murder and rushed into the entry. Cyrus, Nelly and Mr. J. hastened to the scene of the uproar and rained quite a shout at Elder Wiggins dripping appearance. And very soon that gentleman took himself up to his room to remove his attire.

Aunt writes she is coming home next Saturday night, I must see that all household concerns are in a favorable situation. I should be sorry to have my reputation as a housekeeper suffer through my love of frolic. I like to have everybody around happy and like to enjoy myself besides, and I mean to do it. Young folks can't be old folks, and I can't see any harm in being lively if we don't do wrong. Anyway, I don't see why it is worse for one to be wild and full of nonsense than it is for another.

Ellen says she supposes we must get quiet before the folks come and as for the Elder he has a long face to draw on anytime. I have been prescribing Catnip and Laudanum for us all so I guess on that whole we shall be in readiness to receive them in due sobriety.

Frank asked me last night if I shouldn't be sorry to have him leave when the folks came back. I said I did not know as I should, particularly. He said he did not think I cared a cent for him. I told him "I never pretended to." He said "that is a fact" and added that I had a very original way of my own of making sure that nobody cared for me. And as for caring for anyone myself, he guessed I never did or should. Well, I will own up to this in a measure. I hope I am not one of that class of girls who have so good an opinion of themselves that they think that if a young man is decently polite and attentive to them that he surely wants to marry them. I don't mean to be such a conceited specimen anyway.

September 20, 1858

Uncle and Aunt have arrived and in much better health than I expected. Uncle was able to milk the first night. Aunt praised my housekeeping very much. Said my butter looked as good as hers and my pies were full as good as hers, too. In her eyes, this is the highest praise, I suppose.

We had quite a "blow up" the other evening. Frank was here. Ellen remarked something about eggshell cakes which amused the gentleman considerably, and set Aunt to inquiring immediately about what was meant. Frank and Nelly gave quite an entertaining account of that proceeding and though Aunt could not help laughing, still she thought it incumbent upon her to reprove me for imposing upon such a good fellow as Frank. I told her I did not intend to impose on him. I was making custard pies and had some egg shells left and knowing she was economical, I thought I could make Frank eat them. It would be just so much saved but I couldn't get the nuisance to swallow them anymore than the old woman could make her rooster set. However, he cackled well, and I thought that was something. After she found she could not arouse any pity in my heart or make me promise not to cut up any more such capers, she turned the conversation upon something else and harmony was restored for a time.

October 2, 1858

Nelly has had a letter from home and thinks of leaving soon. Last week, we went over to Fryeburg (or rather week before last) to see Susy. We stayed three or four days, had a very good time and a pleasant ride over and back. Fanny was in good spirits and behaved finely. She is a nice old pony and knows her mistress well.

Stuart Bradley said he was coming over to get me in a few weeks to go over and stop sometime at his house. They felt very bad when we came away last time. Mrs. Bradley is pretty lonesome, I guess.

The other night, I met up with Mr. Jordan. He said he wanted me to go up to have a swing, for they had a grand one up to Mr. Frost's. So I told him Nelly and I would go, and that night we went up. Seth and Almira Berry were there and several others. Rob wanted me to swing with him, but I wouldn't. Then Ed Bennett asked me. But I declined as saucy as I could. I was sitting on the stairs, and Mr. J. came and sat down by me. He was dirty from the shop and said if he did not look so nice he should make me swing with him. I told him he needn't think so much of his good clothes. I would swing with him now anyway, to lower his pride. He started up and said will you honest? Yes, honest, said I. So he led me out and as soon as the next couple got out, we took our seats. Leander came along and said he would swing that load, and he did swing us with a good relish. I guess we had the best swing of all.

After we got through swinging, Mr. J. asked me if I wasn't going to singing school. I said I didn't know as there was one. He said there was not, but they talked of having one. I told him I guessed I should go then for I could sing like a Hippopotamus. Then Nelly came along, and he walked down home with us.

December 20, 1858

It has been quite a while since I have written in this book. I have been very busy and so have had no chance. Nelly has gone home and singing school has begun. Also, Stuart has been over, and I have been to Fryeburg and spent a couple of weeks. Singing school began the last of November. There were two nights before Stuart came over, and I went those two.

At recess one night, Mr. Jordan got one of my mittens away from me so when it came time to go to Fryeburg I wanted it. I went up to Mr. Frost's and found Mr. J. watering a horse. He said my mitten was in his coat pocket and if I would go in a minute he would get it for me. I went in and Mrs. Frost asked me into the sitting room and then went out. Pretty soon the gentleman came in and got my mitten but would not let me have it, he said, till I gave him something else to remember me by. So I found a pair of old silk gloves in my pocket and asked him what he would give me for them, while he was hunting in his pockets to see if he could find anything, a piece of white paper dropped out of one and fell on the floor. I picked it up and found half a dozen "Phebes" written on it. "Well, well," said I. "I'll keep this, if you please," and I threw him the gloves and attempted to pocket the paper. But he looked rather confused and seizing my hand said I wasn't fair not even to let him see what it was. I asked him to please let me be for I wasn't used to scuffling for a living and didn't know how. He stopped in a moment and said if I would only show it to him, he wouldn't even snatch it. So I opened the paper. He looked at it, a moment, and then at me and said I might keep it. He could remember that name without having it written down. Then he shook hands with me, and we said goodbye, and I ran home.

That afternoon, Stu and I started for Fryeburg. I had a very pleasant visit but was glad to come back when the time came. They wanted me to spend the winter at cousin Mary's, and Stuart insisted that I should attend dancing school with him. Aunt gave her consent to my doing so, but I am too lazy to dance much and thought I would rather attend singing school. So when I had made a good visit I came home.

Last week I started for singing school again. As I passed Mr. Frost's, he came out and seemed very glad to see me, I don't know whether he was or not. He wanted me to "go in" anyway. He said there were lots of girls in his house, and they saw me coming up the road and told him to tell me to stop and go with them. But I wouldn't go in and after calling me contrary as I could well be and live, he retired, and I went on. At recess my old friend, Mr. J. made his appearance just as Mr. Savage was calling us to order. He and Leander took seats not far from Miranda Potter and me. And though Leander fired roll after roll of lozenges and peppermints in a perfect shower at me, still I wouldn't look 'round, but remained solemn and composed as an Owl at Midday.

I sang a duet "beautifully" Mr. Savage said, which was a great wonder to me, as I was so full of mischief, I couldn't stop to think of singing or anything else. As soon as school was dismissed, Colonel Perley came tumbling over the seats like a great pumpkin as he and said he was going home with me. I told him I was sorry to disappoint him, but I was afraid of his wife. And as I was obliged to sit with her in singing school, I wanted to keep on good terms. He roared like a lion in hysterics, and disappeared.

I put my things on and had just left the door when my "old friend" stepped up and asked if he might carry my singing book home. I handed it to him and by a very sudden performance he took that hand that held the book and put it in his arm. There I was, caught, fairly, but not against my will exactly. He said he wished I was as glad to see him as he was me. I told him that was rather questionable. He said he thought my visit never would end. I said it seemed shorter to me than a visit over there ever did before. When we got home, I stood on the doorstep, and he said "May I?" and I said, "I guess you may." So he took or rather gave me a kiss. I don't know how to kiss. Never kissed a man in my life as I know of. So he didn't get any kiss back from me.

The next night, I went to singing school and came home the same way. Only he said when we parted there wasn't going to be another singing school for a whole week, so he must have more than one, and so he took two, three, half a dozen, or so.

When I went in, Aunt inquired what on earth made me stop so long before I came in. I told her I was kissing my beau. She laughed and wanted to know who he was. I told her I couldn't think of his name, but she would probably find out when she got our invitations, if not before. Uncle had gone to bed and called out that if I had a beau, he should think the world was coming to an end. Especially if I had the same one more than two nights in succession. And if he had got so far as for me to let him kiss me, he supposed he'd have a little job and a large fee and plenty of cake quite soon. I told him I had adopted a new plan, instead of getting sick of the beaux myself I was going to make them get sick of me. Uncle said that was all right but a little dangerous.

I wonder how it would seem to be engaged to a man. I don't think I should like to try it at all, and what more, I never will. If I have got to be married, I will tell the unfortunately lucky man that if he wants to leave at the last moment he may, and I shall wish to claim the same privilege.

January 15, 1859

Some days have passed since last I wrote here. New Year's Day has come and gone again.

Jake Choate invited me to a New Year's party, but I was engaged. Engaged to stay at home, that is. I wish I could think of some likely damsel to recommend Jacob to-- he has eyes like "sarcers" and such a luxuriant crop of whiskers! Only they look as if they were struck with the potato rot. Surely, he would make an excellent match for some one. He would never be bright enough to know whether he was "henpecked" or not.

Singing school continues, and I continue to go, too. Aunt laughs at me occasionally, and Uncle wants to know if it is really a fact that the same fellow has come home with me five nights in succession! Verily, 'tis a wonder to myself. The other night a paper was given me, and when I got home I opened it and found a little heart, with "will you be mine" on it and a verse of poetry. It was directed "To My Mary." I had been tormenting a certain individual 'bout a certain Mary, and he declared *she* wasn't *his* Mary. I didn't exactly know what to make of the heart and verse (the heart was broken), so I wrote some verses in reply. I wrote them in such a way, that if it was meant for a joke he would know that I took it so, and if it was a serious affair, the one who sent it would know I wasn't displeased and his feelings would not be hurt. I would not like to do that.

Then a day or two after, Aunt was hunting 'round among my things and found the paper and opened it and read the note and saw the heart. She was almost crazy and insisted I should write and find out whether it was meant for a joke or not, and as I had some curiosity about it myself, I did so, and got an answer the same night that was definitely no joke. I put that where I guess nobody will get it very quick, and in a day or two I answered it. Aunt tried very hard to find out something, but she couldn't seem to, and so things went on quite quiet for some time.

Last singing school night (which was Saturday). At recess some of us girls got to teasing about the boys. Ansel Fitch began to hint something to me about "my beau" going over to Denmark to a certain "new house" rather often. Then the girls said they wouldn't have such works if they were me. I said it was too bad, but unfortunately my beau likes flapjacks pretty much, and I guessed they treated him when he went to the "new house." They all laughed and turned upon Arthur, who looked at me rather disconcerted not knowing if I was in jest. He didn't say much. I was talking nonsense as usual, and we were all laughing when Arthur turned 'round and walked away. When school was dismissed, I noticed my attendant was rather sober all the way home. He said he was so afraid I believed those stories, and if I said so he never would speak to a woman again--excepting my own self.

January 27, 1859

Singing school has been keeping quite a long time. I guess Mr. Savage thinks I am a very apt scholar. He stayed with us the other night. He said he guessed some of his pupils cared more about going home from singing school than going to singing school. I asked him if he meant me, 'cause if he did I would own right up and say he had told the truth for once. He laughed and said he did not mean me. He meant a certain young man who came in so regular at recess time, and looked so cross that night when he (Mr. Savage) said he was going home with me.

Well, I am willing. Folks should say what is wrong, not hide it. I think it would be very wrong, when I like a certain person and know he likes me, to slight him or treat him with indifference. I would not do that. I think he thinks because he has not had as good advantages as I have or because he has to work for a living that he is not up to snuff. I think he deserves a thousand times more credit and praise for being what he is, than I do for being what I am.

He is just as good as he can be, and I like him, and I am just as willing to own up to that. It is rather hard work to plague either of us, I guess, according to all accounts.

If Aunt or any one beside that old mischief maker, Grand ma'am Frost, could bring anything against his character that might make some difference with my feelings but as to situation and position and education and all that nonsense, I won't hear a word of it. I don't know as I could love anybody. I don't know as I want to. I'm afraid if I should, I never should get over it. And that would be bad. I know he loves me though.

Even without his telling me of it as often as he does. But as for loving back, that's another thing. Anyway, I like him.

March 15, 1859

I have thought a good many times if I ever should be courted how I should behave. Aunt said to me today "Phebe, if you go on in your careless-lively-social-playful way, some one will surely take advantage of it, and his love for you go farther maybe than a modest girl might like." I know I always show right out what I am. If I am cheerful and happy, I act so. I can disguise my feelings pretty effectively if I choose, but I mean generally. I don't mean to do anything forward or rude or unwomanly, and I don't think I have done so. Anyway, I never had the first impolite or improper words spoken to me by any man or boy under the sun in my life. I have lots of friends, and good ones, too, and some enemies. A few enemies I've made, I suppose, because they wanted to be better "friends." But I couldn't help that I have seen girls hugged and kissed in play and did not want the same. I never cared to know what it is was to be hugged. I have put down one truth in this book. And as I always despised kissing (till lately), it was no self-denial to keep from plays which involved such proceedings, but rather a pleasure on my part to be let alone.

Now I don't think I shall take up with my Aunt's advice and be more reserved and cool and dignified, etc. etc. I shall try to do what is right and act myself--and if any man can take advantage of liveliness and sociability to act improperly then surely he is not the man I would want for a husband.

I don't wish any man to go farther than "playing and kissing" until he has a right to, and he can't have a right to till I belong to him wholly. I don't believe anyone expects or can expect anything else. But perhaps I don't understand mankind or womankind so well as more experienced persons may. Anyway, I have my own ideas, and if circumstances require, I can express them "peaceably" if I can, "forcibly" if I must.

March 27, 1859

Oh! There is a new star risen in this place. We girls call him "Harry". We are all "taken" with him, of course. Women are always said to be taken with new things. He comes over here very readily. Fortunately for me, I am not a sentimental damsel. I have the wit to recognize a woman killer. He is quite decided in his attentions, so perhaps I better try and kill him. If there is anything I despise it is a "gentleman coquette," if such a term is allowable. If a man likes the girls, let him be general in his attentions but not try to secure any one girl's affection and then cast that one off. That is perfectly wicked and outrageously mean. Well, my former friend, Jordan by name, thought he would stand aside and watch the enchanting Harry's attentions to me for awhile. I suppose that to be the case anyway, since he was suddenly missing. I presume he wouldn't have stepped aside so easy if he had not known the lordly "Harry" and I would soon fly asunder.

Alas we did! It was at a party, a thing I seldom attend. Our hero Harry tried to drive me to do something I did not choose to do. I am full of mischief and foolery, I know, but I won't impose on and make sport of innocent persons (that, to be sure, don't know a great deal) just to please and gratify those who are a little smarter and think they know more. Besides, my friend Harry, you never can drive me to do a thing. You better have found it out before, if the loss of my friendship makes you feel as bad as you pretend, Sir. Well, when our famous star Harry found that one Phebe Jane would not mind his order, he tried to make that young maiden jealous. Oh, oh, oh, dear, now--two can play at that game and if anyone begins it with me, he always gets beat or plays to the end of his days. Paying attention to others never did bring me 'round and never will. Let who will try it, and when the imperial Harry came and lowered his pride sufficiently to tell me that he exceedingly regretted his flirtations and that I did just right in refusing to play a trick upon and make sport of the person he wished me to and that he "could not help liking me better than he could like any one else," etc., he found a young man by the name of Jordan rather in his way! Our acquaintance was rather "short" but not particularly "sweet," was it Harry?

April 10, 1859

I have just heard back about the Valentine which I sent to my friend, Nelly Fessenden. She does not dream where it came from me. That was a good idea of mine, to send it without a post mark. Everybody laughs at the idea of her marrying Dr. Lincoln because he is so much older, but I rather think she will do just that little thing. He is an "old batch," and I do not know why she fancies him. Still I wish her every happiness if she does marry him.

I think I shall copy my Valentine here. 'Tis not often that I indulge in making poetry, and when I do I think 'tis worthy of a place in this extraordinary work. This wonderfully entertaining journal.

To Nelly

I've lived for many, many years
Uncharmed by woman's wile
Regardless of her frowns and tears
And needless of her smiles

Bright beauty's witching, winning power
O'er me has no control
Wit may amuse me for an hour
But can't enchain my soul.

The pomp and pride of outward show
True bliss can ne'er impart
I seek for that which lies below
I seek for a loving heart

But beauty, wit, and loveliness
I find in her united
And ever since I saw thee first
My love to thee was plighted

I'd bind my lot to thine, sweet girl
And find some calm retreat
And spend the remnant of my days
In kneeling at thy feet

So now my dearest darling one
Whene'er these lines you think on
Remember, love, I pray you do
Your truest friend, John Lincoln.

I don't expect 'tis customary to sign a name to a Valentine, but I thought I should do it just to astonish the young woman. I wonder what the Dr. would think to have such an expressive article as the foregoing attributed to him.

May 7, 1859

More than a month has passed since I wrote in this journal. It seems sort of foolish to write when I have nothing of any importance to put down, and nothing of interest has come under my observation.

I have been reading all kinds of literature lately: red, white and "yellow covered." Our new boarder, Rev. Mr. S.G. Norcross caught me reading a regular blood and thunder novel the other day. He remarked that some young ladies would have considered it their duty to hide it or sit down on it, or do something to get it out of the way if they saw the minister coming. I told him I was glad he found me reading it, otherwise he might have thought me perfect, but now he knew I was a fallible mortal and liable to err!! "Then", said he, "You acknowledge it is an error to spend time so." To be sure I do, said I, but if people always did right and never committed any errors where were the need of the ministers? He laughed, sat down and said, "So you acknowledge you are doing wrong and think it is my work as a minister to convert you. Is that it?" Not a bit of it, said I. I don't consider it wrong to read such books. But I am "foolish" to spend time so. And, if I choose to be foolish, I don't know as you have any right to interfere. And if I thought you wanted to convert me, I think I should be tempted to do it all the more." He seemed rather amused and walked off.

I called after him and asked if he didn't think South Bridgton was a promising field of labor. He said "very" and invited me to go and help him find some flowers to analyze for the school he has in botany. So I went. I like him. I think he is a really good man and a good minister, too. He is homesick as he can be here, though, and I don't wonder. He and Aunt don't get on exactly together. I don't think Aunt is very well-calculated to make anyone feel at home. I would not be as particular as some people are for a handsome fortune. When Aunt is gone, he comes out in the kitchen and sits with me and seems as cheerful and social as can be. But he says he does not dare make himself at home when Aunt is about. She watches him so.

He is one of the sociable ones, and when he gets lonely he has the "blues," I know. I wish his lady, Clara, lived nearer. Then he could be cheered up now and then. The best remedy for low spirits is to move into the state of Matrimony. Only be sure and get the right one to move with you. I don't think he will stay here long. I don't get homesick myself very often but would if I depended on those around me for company. But I am not one of the lonely kind.

June 27, 1859

I am getting quite remiss in regard to writing in this book. Pretty soon, I shall forget to do so entirely. I'm afraid I have so many letters to answer that I get almost tired of writing. My life is marked by altogether too few marvelous incidents and exciting changes to render a journal very interesting but seeing as I have got so far in the book, I will fill it with something.

I had a splendid sail on the pond the other night. Mr. Shaw and Arthur came and invited me. There were several others, but May Perley and I were the only girls. We had a fine time. Mr. Shaw is a very pleasant man. They say he is one of the hen-pecked ones and that his wife treats him very unkindly. If it is so, she ought to be ashamed of herself. He works in the machine shop and boards at the house next to us. We sang during our sail. When we were going home, Mr. Shaw asked if he might come in and have a sing with me sometime. I told him if he wished it he could, but I was not much of a singer. Arthur invited him to come in the next night with him and promised him I should play his favorite tune, "Kinloch of Kinloch" and the "Louisville March" on the piano. The gentleman seemed very much pleased at the idea, and we left him and proceeded home. Arthur and he are great friends. I asked Arthur if I had not better invite Mrs. Shaw to come too, but he said he thought we should have a better time without her. So I said no more. It makes no difference to me.

July 10, 1859

Arthur celebrated Fourth of July by taking me over to his father's. I had quite a pleasant time. They made everything of me and treated me as if I was altogether too good to fare as common folks do. I like them all, especially his sister Mary. She is considerably older than I but very pleasant and agreeable. I think Arthur was perfectly happy. He said he had got his wish at last. He had been wishing for the last six months that he had the courage to ask me to go over there with him, but he said he knew they did not any of them know half as much as I did, and he was afraid I should not enjoy a visit there. I could not help laughing, but I told him education was not everything. If persons made a good use of what advantages they had, that was enough. And as for me, I enjoyed myself much better in the company of those who did not know so very much as some I had seen.

Susy is here on a visit. She and Arthur have had one or two spats. I tell them red heads always strike fire when they come together. Susy thinks I am throwing myself away on Arthur, and Aunt has ventured to hint as much once or twice. I don't think so, to be sure. They say "love is blind," and that's one thing makes me think I can't be in love for I see faults in the gentleman, and I don't hesitate to tell him of them, either. But, on the whole, I think he is better than the generality. If it was not for one trait in his character, I should be very well suited. I suppose I ought not to expect perfection, but still, I am afraid the lack of that one thing will make trouble hereafter.

August 5, 1859

Instead of being a diary I guess this doesn't get written in oftener than once a month. Uncle seems to be growing worse. He is confined almost wholly to his bed now. I read to him a good deal, and we have considerable company, so he doesn't seem much lonesome.

There is one thing that puzzles me not a little, and as this is the place for puzzling thoughts, I will put it down. I wonder if, when folks are married, they care no more for each other than for anyone else. Does love cool off and fly away after a year or two of wedded bliss? If so, I don't care to get married, I'm sure. I have seen husbands and wives who did not seem to care hardly anything about each other, yet they live together as a matter of course. I don't go in for any such thing. If I had a husband, I should try and find one that I could love, and then I should calculate to love him better than everything else in the world. I can't bear these commonplace people. Folks that can like or love everybody, those that can have a smile and a kiss for everyone almost alike. Affections scattered around so widely are not worth much. I love to have folks call me "cold-hearted" and say I am no more "impressible than stone" and all that or even go as far as Frank did, and say he would as "soon think of trying to hug and kiss a wildcat" as me. I like to be thought of so. I've got it in me to love, but as for showing it off to everyone, that's too much trouble.

When I do love anybody it won't be halfway work, but I am thinking I never shall find anyone to love. Anyway, I would like to know if love is expected to die or go to sleep after marriage and must a girl after courting days are over settle down (to speak plainly) into a baby manufacturer and a stocking darner. Glorious occupations!! What sublime enjoyment and untold bliss is unfolded here! Oh, we would be married! Not I .Not I.

Aunt asked me the other day why we did not hurry up affairs. She said there was nothing to prevent our being married, and she thought we better be, if we were going to be. I don't want to hurry. I'm half a mind to back out now. I ought not to think of such a thing as that now, I suppose. It would not be right after he has yet to consider me so confidently as his property. But somehow I can't help hesitating to take the step. I think... Well, I don't know what I think hardly. I don't know as I ought to doubt his love, and yet, well, Aunt says perhaps any love will come after marriage! It makes me think of an abominably ridiculous story somebody told the other day, of a couple who sued for a divorce, and the one they applied to to grant the writings made this very refined and sage reply: "Go along home and go to bed. Even the pigs will learn to love each other by sleeping together." (I don't think this story looks very well here or anywhere else, but if it will do for a minister to tell, it will do for me to copy, though I acknowledge it is in very poor taste to say the least.). It may all be very true, however, but the truth of the matter is I should wish to love my pig before I slept with him. That's all. If I didn't, I don't think I could learn to. But what am I writing all this nonsense here for! I suppose it will look well for me to peruse when I am old!

October 20, 1859

Worse and worse. Almost two months have flown by since I favored my journal with a little nothing. Time and tide wait for no man or woman either. But here, let me see. I've got something fine to chronicle today.

Mr. Shaw has been in half a dozen times to sing, and two or three times for a social call, and his devoted companion is jealous of me! So much so, that she has communicated her woes to several of the neighbors. By some, she is laughed at and by some sympathized with, of course. What shall I do, tell him to stay away? No, I won't. Let folks say what they please. It is nothing to me. I never was alone with the man a moment's time. I usually lay by something interesting to read to Uncle in the evenings, and if Mr. Shaw happens in, he will stay till eight or nine o'clock and hear me read. Is that any harm? The piano is in the dining room. The family always sits there, and Aunt helps us sing. Is that any harm? He says a dozen words to Aunt where he says one to me. And if it is any pleasure for him to call, I am glad of it. I would like to have his wife call, too, if she can behave herself. It don't make any difference what people say. If they are low and mean enough to think he comes particularly to see me, let it go so. Such things are too contemptible to notice. I never spoke hardly a dozen words to him. When he asked me to sing, I have done it and shall do it, and as long as he treats me well and politely, I shall treat him so. So now you wise inhabitants of this sage and upright village, "go it", say all you want to. I never shall take the trouble to contradict anything you may report. If you wish to have it that the married men are in love with me or I with them, so be it. Anything to suit your fastidious tastes. A queer idea you must have of the characters of young women and men, too. I should say but "as you like it." Arthur is somewhat angry about it and was going to act so like a confounded fool, but I told him he should not say a word to him. That would be taking altogether too much notice of the matter. So he said he would not. It must make a man feel mean I should think to know his wife is a fool and vice versa.

November 27, 1859

We have had lots of company lately. I got a letter from Fryeburg the other night, saying that I must go over there, and if I did not come soon, they should send for me. I would like to go. I always have a good time over there. They want me to stop a month or six weeks and "visit everywhere," so they wrote. Uncle says he can't spare me, and Arthur says, "No," very decidedly. I don't know as I ought to go for I suppose I am needed here much more than there. Besides, Nelly reminds me every time she writes of my promise to visit Portland in the spring, and if I go there I can't spend any more time visiting. So I won't go to Fryeburg unless they do send for me. If they take that trouble I must go for a week or two. I hope if Will or Dick don't come over, it will be Stu and NOT Sam. I get along nicely with Stu for I can "sauce" him sufficiently to keep him in his place, but Sam is too soft for everyday use, entirely. I would rather reside in a dish of melted tallow and greasy dish cloths as have him clawing around and spouting off all his foolish compliments. How I should enjoy spending one afternoon sticking pins into him.

Mr. Norcross has left boarding here according to my prophecy. He has taken a room not far from here and furnished it. He takes his meals at Dr. Fessenden's. Miss Clara Carey, the lady he is engaged to, is coming here to teach school. He called the other day and asked me to ride up to Bridgton Center with him, so I went. He says he wants I should get acquainted with Clara, for he thinks we should like each other well.

January 15, 1860

All things go on about so. Frank has been here and made us a little visit. He is spending a week at Mrs. Fitch's with the fair Caroline. Ansel is waiting on a Miss Phebe Patrick of Denmark. Folks say he is bound to have a "Phebe" so he took the first one by that name that he came across. When Sue and I were at Fryeburg, we had our pictures taken, and that villainous Frank has carried them off. They were both taken on one plate, so I don't know as I care so very much, though I have made him promise to bring them back before he leaves the place.

Oh, I had quite an adventure a week or so ago. Mr. Sam. Bradley, Esquire came over from Fryeburg for the special purpose of carrying me over there. He stopped a day or two for a visit. The first day, I was not in the room much. In fact, I stayed out so long that Aunt gave me a real scolding and said I did not treat him with common decency. I told her there were some folks you could not treat with much decency because it did not agree with them. Towards night he proposed taking a walk, and I thought politeness required I should go. So I went. He behaved very well for him, but after we returned he grew rapidly worse, and when I thought best to take myself out of the way about eight o'clock, he was quite inconsolable, so the folks said.

All the next day, he was under my feet the whole time. I could hardly step without treading on him. If he had been a cat there would have been one continual squall. Aunt said I should not go off to bed as I did the night before, for it was not polite. So I agreed to sit up as long as she was in the room. About half past nine she proposed retiring. Samuel was rather slow to depart but finally took up his light and went about half an hour after. I arose to go up stairs but saw his door wide open and light still burning, so I concluded to wait awhile longer. I did so and when I went up, his door was closed.

I went into my room, took down my hair, and got about half undressed, when the door opened, and in walked the old gentleman himself. I was so mad for a moment I could not have spoken to save my life. Then, throwing a shawl over my shoulders, I asked him very coolly what he wanted. He seemed rather confused for an instant and then came towards me. I told him to stop where he was and if he had anything to say, say it now and leave immediately. Then he began, and of all the passionate appeals!! I think his was the most overpowering and impressive the world ever produced. I could not keep from laughing. (I was so angry, I would have cried on the spot if I had not have laughed.) He said if I would only consent to go out West with him and be his forever he would not trade it to be in Paradise. I told him I should greatly prefer he should dwell in Paradise, and I wished he was there that blessed minute. He said he knew he was a fool to try to make me like him. I told him I thought he had acted like one for some time, but if he was willing to own it there was some hope he would recover from his folly.

He called me everything he could think of and said I had tried to avoid him ever since he came over and all the time of his last visit before that one, too. He said I was "stone" and asked if I had not one kind thought or word for him. I replied no. Any thoughts at that time were very far from being kind, and if he stayed much longer, he would find my words were full as far from kindness as my thoughts were. I asked him if he considered it gentlemanly to enter a young lady's room at that time of night without rapping, or in fact to come in at all. He said he was sorry, but he could not catch me alone any other time, and he thought I would excuse it. I said I thought he presumed considerable upon my forgiving disposition if he thought it an excusable offense to act so and that we differed on the subject. Then I reminded him that I was ready for him to leave. I kept growing more and more mad with him. I was cold as ice and my face burned like fire. He got up and came toward the table and said he wanted to light his lamp. I told him to light it down stairs then, for as for stopping one minute longer there, he should not. He begged me to forgive him and wanted I should just shake hands with him, and he would go. I said if he offered to touch my hand I would scream loud enough to rouse the whole neighborhood. Then he left and went to his repose in the dark, I guess.

I spoke to him but once after that before he went home. He asked me the next day when I would be ready to start, and I answered, "never with him." I asked Arthur if he was willing I should go over with Sam when he first got here and I knew he was after me. He said, "Yes, if I wished to." I asked him if he thought I should be willing to have him go riding off with other girls. He said he didn't know. He hoped I shouldn't allow it. I told him, "I was willing, if he wished it." The gentleman did not seem to like that very well.

Aunt blamed me for not going over with Sam, but I can't help that. I calculate to do about as I please alone. My own affairs. I don't care to have any third party (whoever it is) interfere in my concerns. I wonder what Aunt Bradley and Cousin Mary and the famous Georgianna and, in a word, the whole crew over there, will say, because I would not go over. I don't know as I care, though, any great deal what they say.

February 20, 1860

We had a splendid time skating down on the pond the other night. There were lots of us. I did not calculate to go, but after May called for me, Esther came and almost persuaded me to alter my determination to stay at home, and then John Perley and Ed Bennett came up from the pond and said they were getting up some kind of a "spree," and I must go down. So I got ready and went and enjoyed myself finely.

Oh! I hear by way of my Fryeburg correspondents that Sam has returned to that verdant vale and commenced courting Susy with unparalleled devotion. I thought I would just let Susy know that I was aware of how matters stood, so I sat down the other night and wrote her the following Valentine:

"To Susy"

Transcendent Angel! Like the sunshine on the distant hills
The thought of thee my soul with truest purest rapture fills
I see thee in my waking hours and in my dreams thou ist there
Of Nature's many lovely flowers the sweetest and most fair

Yes, loved one, yes, when I'm entranced by music's thrilling tone
The thought of thee comes creeping o'er me, like a spider o'er a stone
Thou art the one bright dazzling star upon my pathway shining
And I am blest, supremely blest, when in thy smiles reclining

I'd ask no other earthly bliss, I'd clasp no other earthly treasure
If thou'lt be mine, Kind Fate has filled my cup with overflowing measure
Then let me fold thee to this heart. I care for naught on earth beside thee
I'll live and move and die for thee and worship still whate'er betide thee

Down on my knees I wildly fall, thy hands imploring Sue
Oh if thou canst refuse me what in thunder shall I do!
       Samuel A. B.

I should laugh, I know, if Sue should take a fancy to his gentlemanship. Well, I won't say a word and see how matters with him turn out. I am going over to Fryeburg before long to give them all "Hail, Columbia" and set them to thinking "what's coming next." I expect Susy will tell me all about how affairs are progressing.

March 29, 1860

I have been over to Fryeburg and stopped two or three days. I did not see much of Sam, though he made himself visible quite often. I don't see as he is particularly attentive to Susy. She told me he thought a good deal of her, judging from his talk. I asked what he said, and she told me some things. Then I asked her if she would promise me to do one thing. After a little hesitation, she said she would, and I told her the next time Sam got into his highfalutin' strains to ask him if he had not said all that once before. She looked a little dissatisfied for a moment or two and then asked if I knew of any girl Sam had been paying attention to. I said it was no matter about that, all I wanted of her was to ask the question. She said she could not think of anyone he ever was waiting on or had shown any attention to particularly lately, but she would say to him just as I told her to.

Not long ago, I had a letter from her. She said they went to walk not long after I came home, and Samuel got to expressing himself pretty strongly, and she asked him if he "hadn't said all that once before." She said he seemed perfectly confounded for an instant and then exclaimed, "What do you mean? Has Phebe been telling you anything?" She said she told him no and asked what Phebe had to do with it. But she could get nothing out of him, only he seemed very quiet, and she insisted I should tell her what it all meant for she knew I knew about it, or he wouldn't have mentioned my name. I have told all I'm going to. I don't know as I ought to have made her ask him that, but, somehow, my love of mischief made me do it. I never will do so again, though. If a fellow is ever so mean and makes a fool of himself, 'tis too bad to tell of it. In fact, I haven't said a word about it. But 'tis mean to hint and set anyone to guessing. If I could not keep from being a fool, I would not want it told of.

April 20, 1860

We are beginning to talk about May Day and to plan for its celebration. We are going to have a queen crowned, then a walk and a picnic. A few days ago, we had a meeting in the High School building to make arrangements and ballot for a queen. Our meeting was called to order by Miss H. M. Peabody, and we proceeded to vote for a queen. Votes after being counted stood thus. Miss M.F. Potter, 9, Miss Mahala F. Perley, 6, Miss P.F. Beach, 12, and Angeline Foster, 3. The next thing in order was for Miss Beach to back precipitately out of that honorable position. Miss Potter having the next number was elected queen. Mr. Norcross was chosen to give a short address and crown her queenship. Then four maids of honor to attend the queen were chosen - Misses M.F. Perley, H. J. Knapp, P.F. Beach, and Jane Brocklebank. After all other arrangements were completed, we agreed to meet once more during the coming weeks and adjourned our meeting 'til that time.

I am really glad my sweet friend is to be queen. I think she will make a grand one. She is just the one to carry it off well. She is to be dressed in white and her four maids in white skirts and black waists with wreaths upon their heads. What a time of Excitement! Oh, dear! I wonder if we shall all live through it. I shall feel like a monkey with a hand organ. I expect that what "can't be cured must be endured."

May 15, 1860

Our May celebration passed off finely. Mr. Norcross gave a short and comprehensive speech. Miranda did admirably and bore her honors with resignation and fortitude. They had a little difficulty in selecting a suitable seat for Mr. Norcross and the Queen to occupy, and I suggested that they should inhabit a huge bunch of sweet briar worked as a throne. My proposals that the royal couple should make a nest in that thorny locality entirely upset the gravity of the gentleman and lady, and they were some time in recovering their former equanimity, but finally they got comfortably seated. We had a fine walk. The tables were well filled.

After the public performances were over, Arthur spoke for another walk, so we went. He was very anxious that the Happy Day should be set. He said Aunt had spoken to him several times about his going to our house to stay, and he did not know as it would be just the thing to take up his abode there till he had a right to. I told him he and Aunt might settle that. I was not particular. I don't believe I was ever made to be married. I don't think I shall like married life. I like him ever so much, but I don't like the idea of being married. I like him as a friend, but I think a woman is a fool to get married and here I am, walking right into it!

I think I must have forgotten the song I play and sing--

"In youth, love's light burns warm and bright
But it dies ere the winter of age be past
While friendship's flame burns ever the same
And glows but the brighter the nearer its cast."

I don't know as I could hardly explain what I mean by a woman's being a fool to be married. I don't mean marriage is a foolish institution, of course. If a man likes a woman, and she likes him well enough to think they could live happily together, they should get married and go on loving each other better and better until they love each other so well there is no room for anything else. That's the way to do matters up, but 'tisn't so generally. When folks get married, they say, I suppose, "Well, we are fairly tied now. The excitement of the thing is all over. All that remains is to settle down into dull, old lumps, laboring to provide for innumerable young brats which are daily expected."

If I could go back and begin again, I would not look at a man or speak to him as long as I lived if I could help it. Not but what I think married life might be and ought to be the very pleasantest lot on earth. But, heavens, earth! What does it often turn out to be!! Well, one thing is certain, a kind of regard for public opinion might induce me to live with a man (if I was married to him) even if I did not care much about him, but never as his *wife*.

I don't mean to write in this again till I have tried the sweets of married life. Then the cares of that new and interesting state of being will prevent my writing in my journal very often, but I can keep account of the most remarkable incidents that occur (if there is anything that happens worthy of note). If not, I will put down, now and then, a "commonplace".

July 15, 1860

Uncle has grown so frail. I nurse him every day, getting him up, washing him, bringing his meals. I can see how he has failed. He is still his usual kind, jovial self, but I can see how hard he tries to hide how poorly he feels. I fear he will not be with us much longer.

I cannot understand Aunt. She avoids going near Uncle as much as she can. If he were my husband, I think I would be with him as much as I could. She stays away and lets me care for him.

Aunt and Arthur are busy making plans for our wedding. I leave them to their plans and tell them to let me know what they want. I don't much care, as I do not think marriage such a prize as to require much effort on my part.

If I must marry, Arthur will make a good enough husband, if one must have one. And if I must have a wedding, I want Uncle to perform it. I think Aunt will have the wedding soon while Uncle is still with us.

July 28, 1860

I thought I would not write here again, till I had exchanged my name for another, but having a little time tonight I take up my pencil and go to scribbling,

Uncle grows more feeble. It is my business to wash him every morning, get him up, and give him his breakfast, and though I don't notice it being with him so much, still I can see that he fails. I don't see how Aunt can stay with him so little. It seems as if I were in her place, I would want to do everything for him myself, or it should be such good care that they would have to get well.

Arthur got quite excited the other night. He said he had been with me now going on two years, and a good part of the time I never would let him even hug and kiss me half what he wanted to. He said he guessed most young couples did not stop at "hugging and kissing." I asked him, "Where they went to then?" He laughed and said, "No matter." He hoped he should get there sometime but did not expect to, before the last of next month.

The other evening, he spent two or three hours trying to learn me "how to kiss." He said he knew I knew how, but I acted as if I did not practice very often. After he had labored a long time to show one how the thing was done, I started up and told him his kisses were altogether too commonplace, and so I gave him one (just to let him know I knew how). He said he would give me a hundred dollars for to get me a "dress to stand up in" if I would give him another just like it, but I told him I couldn't think of it, and I had already got a dress. He has teased me half the time since then to learn him how to kiss, but I can't afford to kiss very often.

August 30, 1860

It is a beautiful day today. It is my wedding day. Hard to imagine. As often as I have written about the perils of marriage, I am surprised to find myself walking right in to it. Aunt is all aflutter with arrangements. It seems my only job is to dress appropriately, be in attendance at the proper moment, and speak my piece. And then I shall be a proper, respectable wife.

Uncle especially asked for me to sit with him awhile this morning. He talked to me about his own wedding day and the early days of their marriage. He said marriage is about adjusting to each other until you find the fit that is right. I think he has had to adjust himself to Aunt's particular ways far more than she adjusted to his. But he loves her despite all her particularness.

August 31, 1860

For one full day I have been a Mrs. I do not know whether I shall like this new profession. Arthur is so sweet to me, and he seems content with his new possession. I have not learned to like married life yet, but perhaps I will in time.

It was most embarrassing on the evening of our nuptials to have Arthur moving into my bedroom. I did not know what to feel when I saw his boots and work clothes in the same room with my dresses and corsets. I suppose it is as Uncle says, and I will adjust.

Even more embarrassing was retiring to "our" bedroom for the wedding night with Aunt fussing about, and Uncle looking both hurt and worried about having a grown married woman in place of his own little girl.

It is a wonder to wake up next to Arthur. He is most affectionate in the morning. It is nice to have someone pet me and call me foolish names. I fear his work will suffer if he continues to linger in the mornings.

September 7, 1860

I have been a Mrs. just 8 times 24 hours! I don't know as I ought to give any opinion concerning the pleasures of married life upon so short an experience. In truth, I might say now it was very agreeably disappointing. Though I should be very happy in the new state of being, still there is no knowing how soon I should begin to sing another song of a different description. I suppose I am enjoying the Honeymoon now. When that is set, I must look out for Matrimonial Breakers on the Dead Sea of Common Everyday Settled Down married life, which is worse still. Well, I ought to be thankful for the honeymoon, I expect. Most folks "honeymoons" turn out to be green cheese and pretty moldy at that, I guess. Arthur seems to be exceedingly well contented with his lot. I tell him I don't think his business will prosper very much if he is as fond of home as he appears to be. But I am glad to have him stay with me. If my husband would always pet me, I would not complain of being a married woman, but you see that is not the fashion.

December 27, 1860

The last month in the year! Well I haven't written here for ever so long now. I might fill a page or two with a detail of "our first quarrel" occurring nearly four months after the nuptial day. Our first and last quarrel. Last I say because I know it is the last.

A few nights ago, Mr. J. was sitting on the doorstep, and I came and sat down beside him. He talked a moment or two, and then he said he "couldn't spend time to act the lover any longer." "Oh, well," said I, "Then, I think you better go up." Something in the way I said it made him turn 'round, and soon he came back and sat down again. "Look here," said he, "Don't you think 'tis time to drop the "lovers" and become 'matter of fact.'" I did not hardly know what he meant, whether he was in sport or earnest but rather thought the former. However, I was in just *that mood* when such things did not exactly suit, so I replied I thought it was high time. As soon as anyone felt love growing less, they better cease acting the lover, and I supposed we had been married about long enough to stop caring for each other much. Then, I arose and went into the house. I felt angry and unhappy and out of sorts, but I kept it to myself till I went up stairs. Arthur had been out all the evening. When he came in, he stopped and looked at me a moment and then went off to bed. Pretty soon it was late. I went up after two o'clock and got ready to go to bed. I sat down on the floor and went to thinking. I thought, "Well, sir, if you want to break me of any wish to be loved, after you have just got me to begin to like it, you can do it. If because we are married, we must cease to care for each other and become 'matter of fact' and follow in the steps of the endless number of couples who care no more for each other than for the rest of man and woman kind, then I might as well begin to learn the lesson, I suppose. But as for *acting the wife* and dispensing with *all* love, nobody can make me do that." My meditations were interrupted by Arthur, who I saw had been watching me for some time, and who called out, "Don't sit there any longer. If you do, I can't stay here but shall be out there with you in less than a minute." I got up and told him I hoped he would be "matter of fact enough" not to do that, that I was just thinking if I mended his clothes and kept them clean and gave him enough to eat and minded him in all things *but one,* I should learn to be "matter of fact," and I would endeavor to drop the lover's life, if it suited him and adapt myself to my circumstances. I looked at him for a moment and then walked quietly and coolly out of the room, went into another and went to bed.

As I lay there and thought of what I had done, I knew I had taken a pretty bold step, but I did not regret it an instant. If he did not mean what he said, he should tell me so. If he did mean it, and wished to turn me off as a "housekeeper" as most married ladies are turned off, I would acquiesce in that. But as for being made use of to populate the world into the bargain, there would be two words to that. And then thinking over matters, I went to sleep confident that it would all come out right some how.

When I awoke it was not very near morning, but the moon was shining bright and I saw somebody dressed and walking the floor in considerable excitement. I rolled over and the moon shone straight into my face. The walking person stopped and looked at me and I at him. He looked almost distracted, and it came over me just about that time that in my fear lest I should be neglected or cared as little for as some wives were, I had made altogether too much of a little thing and had caused more unhappiness than I ought to have done. So I quietly observed to my excited spouse that he did not act very "matter of fact." Then he came and sat down on the bed and we...made all up, as the novel writers have it.

He told me he said what he did more to see what I would do than anything else. But he guessed he never should try it again and instead of his love "cooling off or tiring in anyway it grew stronger every day, and I mean it." He said he thought I was a strange mortal to act so and then go to sleep over it! I told him I hadn't done anything to disturb my rest, and I thought it was "matter of fact" to go to sleep. He said I might have stayed with him and done the same thing. Folks that even dislike each other often kept up appearance because they were husband and wife. I told him I should dread any domestic trouble and suffer as much or more than hardly anyone else *could* suffer in consequence of it, but to keep up appearance or anything else I never would spend one single night with anyone I did not love and who I did not think cared for me. And thus ended our first and last quarrel.

I like married life very well now and expect to like it better and better. Arthur declares he doesn't understand me, and if he did he could make me perfectly happy. I am happy enough now--too happy to last I sometimes think.

February 17, 1861

On the 14th of this month, Uncle died. It was 15 minutes past eleven when he died, and he seemed conscious to the last. Not an hour before he was gone, he asked me to wind up his watch and talked a little with Arthur. Then he turned over and said he would sleep, and he did sleep. The "sleep that knows no waking." When it was all over I could not mourn, for he suffered so much and dreaded death so much that I was almost glad when he got through with all his troubles.

It was his wish that he might be examined so the next day four doctors came and did it. That seemed worst of all, especially as I had to do all the waiting upon them. There were others who could have done it, I suppose, but they thought their nerves would not allow them to go into the room, and, of course, Aunt could not be expected to think of anything at such a time. Because I do not show my feelings like some, but can keep calm under almost any circumstances, folks sometimes think I don't feel. I believe that it is not so, the feeling comes afterwards. Self-control is a very good thing but it almost kills sometimes.

He looked perfectly natural and so pleasant. I liked to look at him. His was the second corpse I ever saw in my life. I fixed some flowers around a little girl once, and she was the only one beside Uncle I ever looked at. Not that I have any fear of a dead person or anything of that sort, for I haven't in the least. But it always seemed to me sort of heathenish to rush 'round a coffin to get sight of what is in it, as if it was some great show as they do at funerals, and I never would do it.

There was a large number at the funeral. Mr. Hawes and Mr. Harris attended it. It seems lonesome, and I miss waiting upon him. Will was up from Brunswick and stayed two or three days. Aunt feels very badly, of course. Arthur is kind and good as ever. If it wasn't for him, I hardly know what would become of us. It seems sometimes as if this was only the beginning of troubles. I don't know what has got into me of late. I am not subject to low spirits but I feel as if everything was dark and growing darker. I think it won't be long before something worse will happen to me. I don't know but I am foolish to have such feelings, but I can't seem to help it. I don't often get "blue," but when I do, it's "black" enough.

February 20, 1861

Without, a leaden sky o'erhead
A brown and barren earth below
Its harvest reaped, its sunshine fled
Waiting its burial shroud of snow
Within my breast a deeper gloom
Than ever fell from sunless skies.
Life's harvest gathered for the tomb
Lost love, Past hopes and broken ties.

Dead blossoms droop from blighted stalks.
While sere and wind-swept autumn leaves
Litter the garden's winding walks
Or lie in heaps beneath the canes
The violets of youth's early spring
The roses of life's summer bloom
Crushed like those Autumn leaves, still fling
O'er memory's shrine their faint perfume

Wild sweeps the wind o'er wood and wold
Like reeds the tall trees bend and sway
Round homes where hearth fires bar the cold
In whose red light the children play
Like reinless steeds they hurry past
I weep on nor rest till morning light;

The moaning of a wilder blast
Is echoing through my Soul tonight.

The last pale rays of daylight fade,
Slow surges darkness' close waves
Above the busy marts of trade
Above the church yard's quiet graves.
A darker night my path enshrouds
And veiled each star-if star there be
Tomorrow's sun shall chase those clouds
But when will morning dawn for me?

July 25, 1861

It is a year next month since I was married, and I would not wish to be any happier than I have been most of the time. There have been sorrows in the time, to be sure, but they would have been much heavier to have been borne alone. Aunt is getting more cheerful. My own spirits have, in a measure, returned and things look much brighter.

I have work enough to do and am getting to be quite a famous housekeeper. We have quite merry times now and then, music of all kinds and dancing of the "first order." Aunt does not like to have me go out evenings and leave her alone. We have had lots of invitations to join parties and rides and such, but Arthur never will go without me, and I want to go ever so much. I know I ought to stay at home if Aunt wishes it, so we don't go much.

October 4, 1861

Ansel and Ed Fitch enlisted today. I am not surprised. All the young men are wild to go. I think Arthur envies them. Neither are married and so feel free to go. I do not know how Mrs. Fitch will manage the farm without them. It seems the fate of women is to labor at home while the men gad about on adventures. I cannot think the Fitch boys will enjoy their sojourn down South.

At church each Sunday, there seems always one more empty place as our men leave. I wonder how many of those empty places will never be filled again. And how many vacant chairs will there be at family dinner tables before this foolish exercise is finished?

I saw Ansel at the post office yesterday. He is full of bravado as he talked to the Old Guard. He claims the war will be over by Christmas, but I fear it will last longer than any of us could imagine.

November 14, 1861

I write in this book a little and then lay it by and have so many other things to think of. I forget all about that I ever tried to keep a journal. I expect I am in what the newspaper Editors would call "a decidedly interesting" condition about this time. Verily, I am ashamed of myself. After all I have said, to be led right into this incomprehensible and unjustifiable predicament! I am actually afraid I shall have to own up that I am a woman, much as I had prided myself to the contrary. What upon earth possessed my estimable companion to cut up such a caper as this, it is most decidedly "matter of fact" and altogether too "commonplace" to suit me. But scolding and worrying will only make a bad matter worse. So I will "endure" with my usual "equanimity." The old gentleman seems quite pleased with the prospect--much more so than I am. I am glad, though, on his account, if he wants it so. He has considerable to trouble him nowadays. He does not get along as well with Aunt as he did with Uncle. I don't believe any man likes to have a woman always dictating around, even if she has a right to. It don't make it any more pleasant. I have had to work pretty hard sometimes to make thing go right and keep peace. I can't do much with Aunt, but Arthur will bear almost anything if I ask him to. This is not very agreeable work for me, though. I would far rather bear it myself than ask him to. I hope, though, matters will mend.

January 30, 1862

Here am I, not fit for much beside writing and not caring to do much of that. Over there on the sofa, lies a bundle kicking and opening some great blue eyes that look quite surprised to find themselves in this miserable old world. I have been trying to convince myself that that piece of property belongs to me, but I can't succeed in doing so. It don't seem that I had any claim to that young specimen at all. Everybody calls him a real beauty. 'Tis certain, he done take after his ma'am if that is the case. He is quite a respectable soul of a baby, though, if one must have one. Weighs nine and a half pounds at 5 days old, and if his adorable pa don't kiss him to death, perhaps he may make quite a man yet. Aunt perfectly worships him, and his nurse says she never saw a baby she loved so well. So I guess among them all, they will spoil him without any of my help. He is a cunning young image, and the Doctor says he is a little too bright. There, I guess, he must take after me. I expect I shall begin to like him as soon as I fairly understand what he is made for. And as soon as I do begin to think considerable of him something will happen to him, I suppose. That is usually the way when folks have anything they love, I believe.

March 20, 1862

Our little baby is gone. I wonder if he was taken away because I did not think much of him. I did love it, after all, better than I thought I did, but I don't wish it back. I think those who don't live to grow up are the most fortunate. Aunt cries half the time. She says she does not think I have shed a tear, but it wasn't because I did not feel like it. I don't cry very easy.

It died of inflammation of the brain, was sick a week, and lived to be just six weeks old.

Arthur takes his loss very hard. I don't think he will ever be contented here now. He can't seem to bear to come into the house and sit down now, though he used to like to do it best of anything. I don't know but he will enter the Army. Though I hope not, it may be the best thing he can do, however, but I don't like the idea somehow.

March 21, 1862

Mr. Knapp brought the pine box for little William today. Aunt lined it with his little blanket and dressed him so carefully. She thinks me hard-hearted for not tending to him myself. I cannot. His cold body reproaches me. I should have loved him, and I did not. Arthur's eyes are nearly swollen shut from weeping. He does not sleep. Only sobs when he thinks I do not hear him. Tomorrow, we lay the baby to rest next to Uncle. They say I must go to the cemetery, but I cannot bear the thought. I know now how cruel life can be, and I doubt I will ever feel carefree for all the rest of my days.

March 23, 1862

My baby rests forever next to Uncle and Mary. It comforts me to think of them together. We walked over to the cemetery following the hearse. The pond is still covered with ice, and snow lies on the ground. They lowered my baby into the cold ground and my heart felt as trapped in ice as the pond. Arthur and I held each other as we stood there surrounded by the graves of our loved ones and neighbors. Aunt could barely stand, she was crying so. Her heart is broken, losing the babe so soon after losing Uncle. When we returned home, I put her to bed with a cool compress for her aching eyes. Then, I suffered through the condolences and pitying looks of our friends and neighbors. At last, they all returned to their homes and left Arthur and I alone. Arthur turned to me to take me in his arms to comfort me. I am sorry to say that I turned away in anger. I do not want comfort. I want my life as it was before Uncle died. Verily, I am in a temper tonight. And I am ashamed of myself for my selfishness when Arthur is hurting so badly.

April 2, 1862

Arthur has enlisted. I did not know it till a week afterwards. He felt so, after he had done it, that he could not speak of it, and it was only by chance that I found it out. I guessed from his appearance that something was the matter. I felt so angry and unhappy at first to think he did it without saying a word to me when he knew I was opposed to it. And I told him I would not write him a word while he was gone. Though I know I shan't keep such a resolution as that.

It is wrong, though, to act so and I won't do it, at least I will try not to. I will be as cheerful as I can, for he feels bad enough and perhaps it is best he should go. Still, I almost know he never will come back again. O hear well--is not a woman a fool to get married? And after all, I think the pleasure I have had is enough to make up for considerable trouble, and it may all come out bright yet. Still I can't but think it is folly to trust any man sufficiently to put your whole happiness into their keeping. Men can't love as women can, I don't believe. They are more impulsive perhaps, but I don't believe their love lasts half as long. Though I don't know, never having had a chance to see. And it is worse than folly to live with one you don't love, so I guess old maids have about the right of it.

April 12, 1862

Letter from Arthur Jordan to Phebe Jordan

Fort Western, Augusta, Maine

My Dearest Phebe,

It has been just a few days since I left you standing on the front doorstep of my parent's house. What a difference those few days have made in my life. I am at the fort in Augusta now with the other new recruits. I have been issued my uniform, and if you could see me, I think you would say I look right smart. Every day we are drilling and training. They have nearly marched the legs off of us. There are rumors flying that we will soon be leaving Augusta to join the 10th Regiment somewhere near Washington, D.C. Imagine that, dear Phebe. Your husband in Washington, D.C. Perhaps I will get to see Mr. Lincoln while I am there. These are exciting times, but I find myself missing you and my folks and Uncle Leander and all the rest.

Oh, dear Phebe, I cannot begin to describe how lonesome I am. I got used to having you cuddled up against me every night, and now I miss that something fierce. I feel so bad for leaving you. I was thinking only of my own grief at losing our baby, and I had to get away or lose my mind. I see now that you were grieving, too. You did not cry when we lost him, so I thought you did not care. I know now that is not true. Oh, Phebe, if you knew every morning the tears I shed out in the barn with my head leaned against our cow as I milked her. It seems I could not bear our loss. I wish instead I had held you and let you cry your pain out. How much more grieved you must have been having carried our babe and brought him into the world. And now, I think of you alone. Your babe buried with Uncle, and your husband far from home. Oh dear girl, what have I done to you?

But I have given my word to go asoldiering, and I cannot back out now. My fervent prayer is that I will be with you again in just a few weeks. Surely this war will not last beyond this summer.

My wife, I am sorry my thoughts are so mournful. I will try to write to you of more cheerful things the next time.

Your affectionate husband,

Arthur

April 17, 1862

Letter from Arthur Jordan to Phebe Jordan

From the Train

My Dear Phebe,

We are on the train heading for Washington D.C. When we marched from the fort on our way to the train station, the ladies of Augusta were out in full force. They gave each of us an orange and donuts as we marched by. They cheered us and blessed us, and it was all I could do to keep tears from spilling out of my eyes. Their kindness reminded me so much of you and my mother and sister. How I miss my dear ones.

We hear that the 10th Regiment is near Washington D.C. guarding the railroads. It does not sound like dangerous duty, so you must not worry about me. I am hoping to see Ansel and Edwin Fitch and some of the other boys from home when we join the regiment.

When the train first pulled out of the station, I was excited to think of all the great sights to be seen. But after the first couple hours, it has all become quite dull. Nothing but the sound of the wheels on the track and the creaking of the car as it sways back and forth. Some of the boys are playing cards and smoking, but I am not. I promised you I would behave as a gentleman while we are apart. I carry the bible you gave me in my coat pocket, and I read some in it every day.

I am anxious to hear all the news from the home folks. Are you still stopping at my parent's house? Is my sister well? What do you hear from Aunt and the Bridgton folks? How is Uncle Leander getting by without my help? Please write often and tell me all that is new.

We are close to the next station, and I must close this letter so I can get it on its way to you, my dear wife.

Affectionately,

Arthur

April 21, 1862

Letter from Arthur Jordan to Phebe Jordan

My Dearest Phebe,

We have arrived in Washington DC, and my what a busy place this is! And very dirty. Much mud every where and dust when it's not raining. We have joined up with the 10th Regiment. I was greatly pleased to run into Ed and Ansel Fitch. They are both well and send their love to the home folks. Albion Johnson is also here. There has been some sickness in the regiment, but for the most part, all are well and the food isn't too bad for army life, I'm told. It is nowhere as good as your cooking, of course. How I would love to have one of your apple pies, piping hot with fresh cream.

I am getting on okay. We cook over a campfire every day, and some of the fellows and I take turns with the cooking duties. How funny you must find that knowing my cooking skills are very poor. I have learned to make a tolerable stew from whatever food we have on hand. When I get home, I will cook you Sunday dinner.

Do not worry about me, dear. I am in no danger. We are guarding the railroads so troops and supplies can get through to the action. I received the stockings you sent but not the strawberry jam. Someone must have heard about your delectable jam and thought to try it himself.

Send your letters care of the 10th Maine Regiment Co. C. My love to all the home folks.

Your affectionate husband,

Arthur

May 5, 1862

Letter from Arthur Jordan to Phebe Jordan

Darling Phebe,

You would not believe how far your husband walked today. We received orders to appear for drill, inspection, and review. We had to march 22 miles to get there! At the close of our inspection, Colonel Miles said, "Gentleman! I have been pleased with the exhibition of this afternoon. Your arms are in good order, you are well clothed and in good drill. You look like soldiers, you are soldiers; the regulars do not excel you." So you see, dear wife, your husband is fit as a fiddle, and you have the colonel's word for it.

It is rumored the regiment is heading closer to the action but do not worry for me. I am well. My love to the home folks and a large measure of the same for you.

Affectionately,

Arthur

May 9, 1862

Letter from Arthur Jordan to Phebe Jordan

Winchester, Virginia

Dear Wife,

We are now in rebel territory. We rode here to Winchester on the trains we have been protecting. Lt. Colonel Fillebrown headed up our journey. Of our regiment, Companies C, E, G, and I are here. Colonel Beal has made his headquarters here, and we are now in General Banks's command and thankful for that.

We left our tents behind, and we are quartering in various buildings. Companies C and I are quartered in an unfinished house, and it is nice to have walls and a roof instead of a leaky tent. Four of our Bridgton boys from Company I are with us, including Ed and Ans Fitch, and we have fine times talking of home.

It is a big change for us here. We are in rebel territory now. The women of Winchester are cold and bitter towards us. When regiments march by, one woman opens her windows and plays

Dixie on her piano. If one of us sits on a doorstep, the woman of the house will send her servants out to wash up the spot as though we are filthy. One woman dropped her prayer book on the way to church. One of our boys picked it up and handed it to her, but she gave him a scowl and refused to take it.

The women of this town show no manners. They will not walk under the stars and stripes. They scowl at us when we walk by and switch their dresses away from us as though we are diseased. This behavior is from the finest ladies who you would expect to know better. We are treated differently by the poor whites. They have been our friends every where we go. At least our soldiers have showed better manners to the "ladies" of Winchester than they have shown to us.

A few days ago and about three miles from here at Kernstown, the rebel general Jackson attacked our forces, but General Banks was able to fight them back. The women of Winchester were constantly jibing us that "Stonewall" was coming, and we would be driven out of the town. They were busy cooking all day long in preparation for the rebels coming.

I am well, dear Phebe, and missing you as always. Write to me please about all that is happening with the home folks. We all miss home so much. A kind word from true ladies is very much desired by us all.

Your husband,

Arthur

Phebe's Diary

May 17, 1862

I am stopping at Denmark now. They are all very kind. It seems as if Mrs. Jordan could not do enough for me. Arthur went three or four weeks ago. We each tried to be cheerful but could not seem to make out very well. I hope it is all for the best, but I think it was wrong for him to go under the circumstances. And I don't think folks ever do wrong without suffering for it sooner or later. I took back my assertion that I would not write and promised to do so after he begged so hard.

I had a letter from him the first week of his stay in Augusta. If he is going to write such homesick letters, I shan't hardly know how to answer them and yet write cheerful, but I can try.

This place does not seem very much like home, for they are all comparative strangers to me. But I am as well contented here as I should be anywhere now, I suppose.

Arthur writes that he shall certainly be back in three or four months. I guess I should wait here again till he comes, if that is the case. He keeps writing such homesick letters that I can't seem to keep my spirits up.

May 23, 1862, Friday

Letter from Arthur Jordan to Phebe Jordan

My darling girl,

You will be most amused to know that two of our Company, Corporal Knight and "Doby" Newbold who is a printer's devil have got up a newspaper. We went to the former location of the Winchester Republican which had been ransacked. We swept up the floors and picked out, washed, and sorted the type, and the first (and last) edition of our paper was published on May 23rd. I say it was our last edition because our day got quite interesting after that, and I think we will soon leave this place.

We heard we were finally going to get our pay and the paymaster was having us sign our pay rolls in the church, when a man came in saying a cavalry man had just rode in saying there'd been a battle at Front Royal and our men were all cut up. Front Royal is about 20 miles. Men on horses and mules started rolling into town telling woeful stories of the fight. Some said the rebels were right on us. There was a lot of confusion before things got sorted out. Our colonel sent word for us to get ready for a fight. Last night, that same colonel had told us to lay in a stock of white gloves for our inspections. One of our soldiers wanted to know if we should be wearing our white gloves. We all took up the query in jest saying, "Every man put on his white gloves." With all the excitement and laughter we "turned in" at a late hour.

I received two of your letters yesterday and was much cheered by the news from home. I expect we will be moving out soon, and I do not know when next I will have one of your delightful letters again. But, Phebe, please keep writing to me. I miss you and my folks so very much. Your letters remind me of my life back home, and I pray that soon this war will be done and I will be sitting down to dinner with you, talking of homely details.

Your loving husband,

Arthur

May 25, 1862

Letter from Arthur Jordan to Phebe Jordan

Darling wife,

I write to you to let you know I came out of our first fight all right. You need not worry about me. Colonel Beal sent our entire company out commanded by Capt. Jordan. Later on, Captain Furbish brought Co. I out to reinforce us. A scouting party came back with word that the rebels were coming. Capt. Jordan marched us back towards Winchester since he felt we were too far from the city, and we were not in a good defense position. He had us set up two miles out of town by the toll gate behind a pike wall. Every thing was quiet til about eight or nine o'clock around twilight when we heard the cracking of pistols coming towards us.

I hope you will not think less of me when I tell you that I was some afraid. My heart was thumping and my knees were shaking, but I wasn't alone in that. We were going into our first battle in the dark with the rebels making dreadful noise. I'm sorry to say that during the fight some of our Company C men were wounded. Company I came out of it all right, so if you see Mrs. Fitch tell her Ansel and Ed are all right. Everything turned out okay for us. Capt. Jordan is an able leader, and he got us through our first battle with much credit to him. Ed said he heard we emptied 73 saddles in the skirmish.

When the battle was finally done, we all enjoyed a hearty breakfast of baked beans. So, dear Phebe, your husband is a real, battle-tested soldier now. If I had my choice, it would be my last battle. I do not enjoy this soldiering life.

Yours affectionately,

Arthur

May 27, 1862

Letter from Arthur Jordan to Phebe Jordan

Dearest Phebe,

I do not know how quickly news of our latest battle will reach you, so I wanted to send a letter to you now to let you know I am doing fine, although it has been a rough patch for us. There was a strong battle at Winchester. We do not know why we were not called to fight as we were ready. Colonel Beal never received an order for us to go or stay. On Sunday, the 26th at around 6 or 6:30 in the morning, we started to see crowds of wounded soldiers and a confusion of stragglers and fugitives from the battle. Colonel Beal decided to take matters into his own hands. He formed up our regiment, and Companies C and I were in the center of the line of defense. We began hearing tremendous volleys to our right. This was followed by first a few stragglers coming towards us and then a crowd, then a mob. Every panicked soldier told a like tale, that being the rebels were right behind them, and we'd best skedaddle. Once the mob was through, we waited in terror for the rebels to attack us. And we waited.

At 7 o'clock, Colonel Beal ordered us to shoulder arms, right face, and forward march away from the rebel forces. We did as directed, but it is a hard thing to march calmly when all others are running pell-mell. It is difficult to resist breaking and running, but we held steady. The saddest part was leaving behind all our baggage, clothing, tents, food, all gone. We also had to leave behind some of our men who were sick and in the hospital.

We barely made it out of Winchester, we found out later. The Rebs had three sides of the city surrounded. From there it was a whole lot of marching. We marched "quick time" and did our best to stay in formation even though we waded through a swamp. Our shoes got filled with water and some very pungent mud.

At some point, the rebels began firing shells at us. We had not heard the terrible whistling shriek or seen the brilliant explosion before. It was exciting and terrible. We were ordered to move a "double quick" and were all happy to oblige. Some were wounded, and their screams were horrible to hear. I wish I could spare you these details, Phebe, but you made me promise to tell you all.

We were headed for a place called Bunker Hill about eight miles out of Winchester, and to get there had to cross a small river. By then, every one was getting tired from all the marching and trying to stay in formation. We were marching through fields and woods until we were able to take to the pike. Discipline was starting to fall apart.

When it seemed the enemy had stopped pursuit, the Colonel ordered us to break organization so we could pick our way along with less fatigue. Some made better time that way, some got on board wagons, and some decided to confiscate horses and wagons from barns and stables along the way.

Every where we looked was wreck and ruin. We saw a number of Negro men, women, and children hurrying away from Winchester with great fear on their faces. We marched thirty five miles in fourteen hours before arriving at the Potomac River. We suffered much, but we were touched by the kindness of many of the good people from Martinsburg to Williamsport. Many of them came out and gave us food and water. That is a kindness I will always remember.

That night was the first time we had to sleep out in the open air. It was only a few degrees above freezing. Most of us had to drop our knapsacks on the retreat, so we had no blankets or overcoats. It was a long cold night. To add to our miseries, our feet had more blisters than good skin, and we all ached from our exertions. It was the longest night of my life.

Phebe, this soldier's life is too hard, and I regret my enlistment every day. Were I of a different ilk, I would leave now and make my way back to you. When I think of how I enlisted to escape my grief over William's loss, I see how big a fool I was. I traded one grief for another, and now I am so far from home, I wonder if I will ever make it back. Forgive me, please, for my maudlin thoughts. I do not mean to burden you. I just feel so very lonesome tonight, and my longing for home fills me with an ache far worse than the ache in my bones.

Your poor husband,

Arthur

May 30, 1862

Letter from Arthur Jordan to Phebe Jordan

Dearest Phebe,

It has been a couple of days since we retreated from Winchester. That night when we had reached the Potomac about half of our army had crossed to the Maryland side, leaving about half on the Virginia side. In the morning, we were unsure of where the rebels were, and those of us on the Virginia side were determined to cross over. Those on the Maryland side did not know if they should stay where they were or cross back over to Virginia. There was a great deal of difficulty and argufying since the ferry boat could not take us all. It looked like a major fight was going to break out among our own soldiers unless order could be restored.

General Banks was called upon to come to the landing. He made us a fine speech praising our patriotism and courage. He said he was very satisfied with our performance under the most trying of circumstances. It was one of the finest speeches I ever heard, and I wish I could have got it down word for word. The general said he had received a telegraph saying a large army was sent from Washington to protect us so we had ample time to cross. We gave nine cheers for the general, and all waited his turn for crossing.

We heard horrid stories that day of the Rebels butchering our wounded, and the women dumping hot water on our men and firing pistols at them as they retreated. We heard the Rebels had boarded up our hospital in Winchester, set it afire, and shot any of our boys who came out.

We have been waiting for word of those of our number who are missing after the retreat. Some have turned up, but many more are still missing. Phebe, I have to tell you that one of the missing is Ed Fitch. We can only hope and pray that he is delayed in catching up to us. Please tell Mrs. Fitch when you see her that we are keeping a look out for him. Ansel came through all right, but he is right worried about his brother, as you can imagine.

I have received no letters for some time now. I am hoping the mail will catch up with us soon. A word of comfort from home would mean so very much. My love to you and all the homefolks.

Arthur

June 5, 1862

Letter from Arthur Jordan to Phebe Jordan

Darling Phebe,

The regiment is in Martinsburg and has received a warm welcome from the residents. Today we finally received our pay for March and April. I am enclosing it all for you save what I might need, which is not much right now. We have been given clothing for the summer and packed up our heavy dress clothing.

We have heard the terrible news that Ed Fitch has been captured by the Rebels and is a prisoner at Belle Isle, a prison at Richmond. We do not know his circumstances other than that, so if his family has heard anything, please let me know. Ansel is distressed, as you may guess.

I received two of your precious letters today and am happy to hear all is well at home. It brings us all great comfort to share good news from home. I think we will be marching again soon.

Arthur

Phebe's Diary

June 8, 1862

A beautiful Sabbath day. I attended church with Mrs. Jordan and Mary. The congregation here is so very warm and caring. They have welcomed me with open arms into their midst. Though Denmark is not home to me, it is a fine village, and the church reminds me much of my own in South Bridgton. It is a lovely place to be if I must be away from home. But still, I do not feel truly a part of this community. It has nothing to do with the people. They include me in all the usual goings on. It is just that I long to see the familiar Sunday faces of all those who have known me since I was a little girl. I wonder how long I shall stay here.

June 15, 1862

I went over home for a good visit. Aunt was most happy to see me. She has been lonesome since I have been gone. I slept in my own room again and almost felt like the girl I used to be. Almost, except that Arthur's things are there. For all my unwillingness to marry, I find I miss him every day. His barn coat was hanging on a peg in the ell. I confess I pulled it close to me to see if any trace of him still lingered there. And though I never cry, I wanted to just then. It seems so unfair that a girl gets used to having a husband and then has to give it up so soon. It was hard to leave Aunt to go back over Denmark. She takes on so when I go. But we think Arthur will come home soon, and I feel I must stay on until he does.

June 16, 1862

Letter from Arthur Jordan to Phebe Jordan

Dearest Phebe,

The past couple of weeks have been uneventfully eventful. Much marching and movement of troops, some skirmishes, but nothing of great important to tell you. One decidedly unpleasant detail has been that we are all infested with lice. We also learned on marching back through Winchester that the hospital had not been burned as we had heard, and most of the stories told were untrue. The women of Winchester continued to scowl at us in a most unpleasant manner, but we were there just a short time, so it was of no concern.

Yesterday, on the Sabbath, we had inspection and review. It was to be held on Saturday, but the heat was so intense, it was postponed. Many men fainted in the heat, and although I am used to the heat of the forge, I felt this heat quite intensely.

You asked about my homesickness. Most of the time, we are busy with marching or cooking or cleaning gear, and I am able to live in the moment. The other men are good company, and we watch out for each other like brothers, so I do not feel so alone as I first did. It is at night when the homesickness sets in. When all is quiet, it is then that my thoughts turn to our dear home. I picture us then with Aunt nodding by the fire, her knitting in her lap, and you reading to me or telling me some amusing story about a neighbor. I miss the way you make me laugh. In truth, there is little reason to laugh here, surrounded as we are by death and uncertainty and fear. I miss the simplest things. Being able to walk over to the blacksmith shop in the morning without worry of shells and gunfire. How much for granted do we take our everyday liberties. The peacefulness of our little village. The friendliness of our neighbors. What I would give to ride to church with you on a Sunday morning and sit in our pew listening to a sermon or joining in a hymn. I treasure each and every day of it all now. I did not know how grand a life we had until I left home. Oh Phebe, to see it all again just for a day is my most treasured dream. I wonder if you will still like me as you used to. And if you would let me kiss you even a little like I used to do. You are my best dream and my first thought upon waking in the morning.

I am always your loving and affection husband,

Arthur

July 4, 1862

Letter from Arthur Jordan to Phebe Jordan

Virginia

Dearest Phebe,

It is the glorious fourth today. We celebrated by ringing the courthouse bell in Front Royal. Some of the men shot off muskets which earned them a reprimand. I wonder what you and the home folks are doing to celebrate the day.

The past few days, we were on a reconnaissance mission into the Luray Valley. Phebe, I should love to show this part of the country to you. It is most beautiful. It is at the base of the Blue Ridge. It reminds me some of the White Mountains, but the mountains here are not so fierce. Whenever we halted on our march we gathered and feasted on cherries and mulberries. It is a bountiful, good land.

During our mission, it rained two or three times and owing to the loss of our gear during the great skedaddle, we did not have our rubber cloths and so wore our clothes wet.

We have been hearing many rumors about the taking of Richmond. I wish the rumors to be true. To capture the Rebels capitol would surely shorten this war and speed my journey home.

I continue on quite well, other than the usual trials of marching and camp. We hear we are to move out again soon. Hoping that your letters catch up with me soon. I miss your stories of home. What would I do without my dear wife to cheer me?

Your loving husband,

Arthur

July 13, 1862

Letter from Arthur Jordan to Phebe Jordan

Virginia

Dearest Phebe,

A wonderful day! We had a church service for the first time in quite some time. We received mail at long last. I had five letters from you, two from sister Mary, and three from Mother. I will not read them all at once, or so I tell myself. I want to savor them.

We have passed some rather pleasant days recently. It was a regular picnic. We were camped out in a grand forest, the likes of which I have never seen, even in Maine. We had shade trees to keep us from suffering too much of the heat. We had abundant rations and more cherries and blackberries than we could eat. The woods were full of our laughter and the music of our bands. It is the happiest moment I have had since we were first married.

Our pleasant interlude did not last, of course. From our picnic, we moved on towards Warrenton through some country that has been terribly devastated by the war. We crossed the Rappahannock River at Waterloo. We camped a couple miles outside of the village and stayed there about five days. We had been ordered to subsist on local rations, so we helped ourselves to all the Rebel sheep and pigs we could find. We found the women of Warrenton to be much like those of Winchester and did not find them to our liking, and they returned the sentiment.

Darling wife, please keep writing to me. It is all that gets me through sometimes. Just knowing you are thinking of your boy far away keeps me putting one foot in front of the other.

Your husband,

Arthur

July 22, 1862

Letter from Arthur Jordan to Phebe Jordan

Virginia

Dear Wife,

We finally had another payday, and since there is nothing here to spend money on, I am sending it all to you.

A few days ago, we marched out towards Culpeper. We marched to Waterloo and Amissville and then were told to march back to

Waterloo, where we camped. We had a terrible thunder storm, and all got soaked. We marched back through our picnic grounds and ended up back at Warrenton. This round the barn, marching makes us all exasperated, and we were wet to boot, so you can guess how cheerful we all were. To add to our woes, General Sigel had ordered his mule trains to Warrenton for supplies, and we had mule mud splashed on us for miles. That night, we were tired, muddy, wet, and roasting in the hot temperatures.

From there, we marched up a high hill above Washington Court House, and we discovered an unthreshed wheat field. We all lay down and rested in comfort for a time. We stayed in that camp for a few days and found cherries and food enough to get by. The view from that hill was both beautiful and useful. We could see for miles. We had good neighbors for company--the 2nd Massachusetts and their fine band which was almost as good as ours.

I have a story that I think you will enjoy, and you must tell it to Uncle Leander in your funny way. I know he will roar with laughter. Sunday, we had a church service. During the sermon, some Connecticut boys decided to round up the loose mules and herd them back and forth at the back of the service. The mules got fed up and gathered near us looking for all the world as though they were following the parson's every word. It looked as though they might get religion. But then, Chandler blew his cornet to give us the key for the last hymn, and the mules started to sing. Such braying and noise you never have heard. They bucked and whinnied and snorted and took off out of the service like the devil was on their backs. Well, we tried to hold in our laughter, but before long we were braying as loudly as the mules, and the poor parson had to end the meeting.

Dear wife, I hope you are well and that Aunt's poor eye is doing better. Please write more about what the home folks are doing, I miss them so.

My love to all and a large measure to you,

Arthur

July 31, 1862

Letter from Arthur Jordan to Phebe Jordan

Culpeper, Virginia

Dearest Phebe,

The regiment is once again in Culpeper, and there is a change in the army. General Pope has taken command, and our troops here are now called the Army of Virginia. There seems to be a gathering of regiments as though a major campaign is under way. The men do not care for Pope, finding him to be too full of himself. The only good news about this is the Rebels hate him even worse. We are told now that we are to deal more harshly with the Rebels. We can take their property and food. We're also told we must take their food because we will not be receiving regular rations. I am hoping still we will receive new clothing since we are so ragtag now as to be an embarrassment.

Also today, the quartermaster has taken away our Sibley tents and given us "dog tents" which are far smaller. It feels as though we've been moved out of the main house and into a lean-to, but perhaps we will come to like them. I do not know. I think we will be moving out soon. We hear there is a load of clothing and shoes coming soon, and I am glad of it. My shoes are worn through, and my trousers are beyond patching.

I wish I could be with you today. My dear wife is turning twenty-seven. You are getting to be quite a matronly age. I will scarcely recognize you when I see you again. I know you will not recognize me. I am a dusty, ragged, decrepit old soldier now. My dear wife, it seems so very long since I have seen you, but when I stop and count the time, it is only three months I have been gone. Next month, we will have been married just two years. You cannot know how much I long for those early days of our marriage. Uncle was still with us, and we had not had the grief of his loss or the loss of our babe. It seems we were young then, and too soon we are old.

This war has caused more harm than good, I think. So many lives torn apart. So many lives lost. So many widows and orphans. When I think of it, my heart breaks. Some day this war will end. Surely it must. I want to think that I will come home, and our lives will be like they were before. But somehow, I know things will never be the same. We have all suffered too much, seen too much. At times, I wonder if I will ever make it home. It seems so very far away from the life I am living now. I feel it all slipping away from me, the goodness and the memories, and I fear I will never hold you in my arms again.

Forgive me, dearest. Forgive me for being so down. Forgive me for leaving you as I did. My spirits are low tonight, and I long to be home with you and far from this terrible war.

All my love to you always,

Arthur

August 8, 1862

Letter from Arthur Jordan to Phebe Jordan

Dearest Phebe,

I write you in great haste. This large army is moving out within the hour, heading south of Culpeper. Rumors are flying that a large mass of Rebels is gathering a few miles away towards Orange Court House. I do not know what the days ahead will bring. I fear we are in for it. The weather is excessive hot, and the roads are sure to be dusty as all get out. At least we have been given new clothes and gear so we will look right smart before the dust settles on us. If the rumors are true, and we go to battle today or tomorrow, I do not know when I shall get a chance to write to you again. I will write as soon as I am able.

My love to you always,

Arthur

Phebe's Diary

August 10, 1862

We hear the 10th was in a terrible battle at a place called Cedar Mountain yesterday. We are waiting for word that Arthur is okay. I am feeling so anxious. The reports we are hearing say the 10th had many wounded and quite a few casualties. Mrs. Jordan has taken to scrubbing the floors to relieve her worries. I am longing for the comfort of home but cannot leave here until I know that Arthur is well.

August 15, 1862

Mrs. Fitch received a letter from Ed. He is alive! He was taken prisoner after Winchester and has ended up at a prison called Belle Isle on the James River in Richmond. His letter was very short, but it brought such great relief to his mother and Cal.

I have heard nothing still of Arthur. He has not been on the killed or wounded lists, so I hope he came out of it alright.

August 17, 1862

Days have passed, and still there is no word of Arthur. His name has not on the killed or wounded lists that so slowly make their way north. Mr. Jordan goes to the post office every day hoping for news from Arthur. Each day, he returns empty handed. Mrs. Jordan tries to keep our spirits up, repeating each day, "No news is good news. You'll see." We sit at the dinner table each night without speaking. Each of us sunk in gloom, and no one has much to say. We wait, and we worry. Every wagon that passes by draws our attention. We catch our breaths and look up expectantly, then let the breath out in a sigh as the wagon continues on.

August 20, 1862

Two days ago, Mr. Jordan returned from the post office with his hand cradling his coat pocket as though protecting a stray kitten. His face was pale. I was standing at the kitchen counter and wordlessly, he came to me and handed me a letter in unfamiliar handwriting. I took the letter gingerly from his outstretched hand, staring at it as I felt the blood run out of my face.

My hands trembled as I opened the letter, and the outside world seemed to fade away. Time truly seemed to stand still, and I felt as if we were all waiting. Waiting to see how our lives would change. Was Arthur alive or dead? If he was alive, was he wounded? Was he a prisoner? Such important questions would be answered, and the future path of our lives would change forever because of the content of that slim, travel-stained missive. I opened the letter and found the following.

"Mrs. Jordan--Dear Madam, It becomes my painful duty to inform you that your husband was killed in action on the 9th of this month during the engagement at Cedar Mountain. He fell while bravely fighting for our country. He was a noble solder and true man, and while we deeply sympathize with you in your loss, we sincerely mourn our own. If there is any thing I can do for you, do not fail to inform me and I will oblige.

Very respectfully your friend,

W. P. Jordan

Captain 10th Maine Volunteer Company C"

Although weekly, and I might say daily expecting such news, still I cannot realize it, now it has come. I do not and cannot believe it. I must write to that Capt. for more particulars.

August 23, 1862

I am back in South Bridgton now. It seemed like the best I could do now that they say Arthur is gone from us. We are in deepest mourning. Aunt is insisting on all the usual proprieties. I do not see how it matters. Everyone in this village seems to be wearing black. Every home seems to have an empty chair, and sometimes more than one.

Verily, I do not believe Arthur to be dead. Aunt thinks I am hiding from the truth. She insists on going on with a funeral service. I will not go! Not even for a minute! She may make whatever arrangements she feels she must without my help.

Aunt is so angry with me. She tries not to show it, but I know she is. She cannot see what I know to be true. Arthur is not dead, and I will not bury him until he is. The neighbors are looking at me as though I have lost my mind. I know I have not.

August 25, 1862

They preached Arthur's funeral service today in South Bridgton. I did not go. Right up until the last minute, Aunt was trying in her firm and gentle way to get me to go. I would not. I will bury Arthur when he is truly dead. I am still waiting for word that he is alive, and I know it will come. I feel the neighbors looking at me. Some look upon me with pity, which I cannot bear. I know others whisper that I have lost my mind.

September 15, 1862

I am at a loss as to what to do with myself. I wait for a letter telling me that Arthur is alive. Every day I go through the motions of housekeeping. Aunt finds me biddable, doing all she wants me to do. Still she watches me, worrying about me. I do not know how to explain to her what I feel. I know to my very core that Arthur is alive. I wish I knew where he was. I imagine a hundred different scenes. Arthur lost in rebel territory. Arthur wounded on the battlefield. Arthur held prisoner. Arthur in hospital with a head wound. I do not know where he is, and that haunts my dreams. I have grown thin these past few months. My gowns hang on me like a scarecrow's rags. My heart skips a beat every time someone comes to the door. I think it will be Arthur. I look for him every day. The world has buried him, but I will continue to hold out hope that I will see him soon.

October 26, 1862

Arthur is alive! I knew it in my soul, and now a letter has finally come. The letter was written for him by some kind hand. He is in a hospital in Washington D.C. He was gravely wounded at Cedar Mountain and taken prisoner by the rebels. I do not know the details of how he came to be in Washington. All I know is he suffers from his wounds and the poor care he received at the hands of the rebels. I must go to him. I fear he will die ere I get to him. I leave tomorrow early for Nell's in Portland. From there, Uncle Samuel will get me on the train for Boston. I heard Mr. and Mrs. Jordan also received a letter. They must be overjoyed with the news, as am I. Aunt is collecting delicacies from the church women to take to Arthur and the patients. I can scarce believe that I'll soon be by Arthur's side. Oh, the miles in between. I wish I could fly!

October 28, 1862

I am at Nell's this afternoon. She welcomed me with open arms and is overjoyed to hear of Arthur. Uncle Samuel has made all the arrangements. The cousins are coming to dinner here at State Street. All the cousins who are near, that is. William, Sam, and Joe are all away fighting. Cousin Pitt is in Washington. He has promised to meet my train and take me to the hospital.

October 30, 1862

I am on the train and on my way. I can scarce believe all that has happened in the last few days. I have gone from mourning to rejoicing. I threw off my black crepe. I am wearing the pink muslin dress and straw hat Arthur first saw me in. The weather is chilly, so I needed a cloak to cover it, but I do not care. I thought the train ride would be exciting, but after the first few miles, I find it dull and exceedingly dirty. The cars creak quite loudly, but the swaying of the ride is not unlike a carriage ride. The wheels on the track sound to me as though they are saying, "Hurry up! Hurry up! Hurry up!"

October 31, 1862

Cousin Pitt met me at the train station and took me straight to the hospital. He was so kind to me. Having a Senator in the family has made getting around Washington much easier. I wouldn't know how to go about getting around without him.

Arthur is very sick. I fear he will not live. He was wounded in the arm and chest. He lay in a wheat field after the battle for two days in the heat. When the rebels took him, they piled him on a wagon with other wounded men. He was sent to the same prison as Ed Fitch at Belle Isle. Ed and the other members of the 10th that were there gathered together shared a tent and any food they could get.

I hear tales from the men of the horrors they experienced at Belle Isle, and I can scarcely take it all in. The men were all infested with lice and fed very poorly. Mostly a little rice made with water right from the James River. Sometimes it was a chunk of moldy bread or a bit of boiled beef. With such poor conditions, Arthur's wounds would not heal. They began to fester, and he developed a terrible fever. The men all helped each other, and I am proud of our boys from home.

Finally, word came that they were to be paroled. That meant a fourteen mile hike to get to the ships. Ed Fitch started out walking with a friend, but the friend left him behind when he couldn't keep up, and so Ed joined arms with Arthur and two others they knew, and they held each other up until they got to the ships. Arthur was put on one of the hospital ships with the sickest ones.

From there, he was taken to the hospital. The doctors do not think he will keep his arm and both wounds still fester. He is often delirious with fever. He recognized me but in his delirium did not think I was real. He knows now that I am here, and I will not leave him.

November 1, 1862

The doctors want to remove Arthur's arm. They say gangrene has set in, and he will die otherwise. I cannot bear the thought, and I do not know what the best course is. Without his arm, he will no longer be able to blacksmith. Keeping his arm means sure death. I can see he has grown even weaker just in the time I have been here. His fever is worse, and I do not think he knows what is to be done which is a blessing.

November 2, 1862

Arthur is gone. He died early this morning. The infections in his body were too strong for him to fight. I was with him at the end. He had a moment of lucidity before he went. He looked at me and spoke my name and gave a little smile. I stroked back his soaked hair from his face and smiled at him. I could not speak, but I showed my love through my eyes. He died then. With that small smile on his face.

I looked down on all that was left of him, and I wept for the loss of him and all he was. I am so angry at this war and what it has done to us all. When I look at Arthur and see how wasted his body is. The eyes sunken and the flesh gone to skin and bones. And I look at the other men around us in the hospital and see the suffering, and hear them crying and moaning from their wounds, how I hate, hate, hate this war.

What use is it for a mother to nurture a son within her, to raise him up to be fine and upstanding, to put all that love into turning him into someone to be proud of, and then to waste him, snuff out his life so senselessly. Oh, we cannot help but pay for this when the time of judgment comes.

I must write to his parents and sister to tell them of this loss.

November 3, 1862

I buried Arthur today. I longed to take him back home with me to be buried with Uncle and our babe. The cost was too much. We laid him to rest in the Soldier's Home cemetery on the grounds of President Lincoln's summer home. He is surrounded by other soldier's there, and I feel he rests honorably. Cousin Pitt attended the graveside service with me, and his presence gave me strength for the ordeal. A minister said a prayer for us, and we each tossed a handful of dirt into the grave. I truly am a widow now. I can not fathom it yet. I believed Arthur would return from the war, and we would take up our lives where we left off. Oh, but then too, a part of me doubted he would return after he left as he did.

I am stunned by the changes in my life in the last year. My husband and babe both gone. I am alone. I am far from my home and all that brings me comfort. Still I cannot cry. I believe there is a part of me that is broken and beyond repair.

Tomorrow, I shall leave Arthur and take the train North. It is a desolate feeling to leave behind the one who taught me the joys of married life. I feel I am leaving my youth behind on the dusty roads of Washington. What joy can life hold for me now?

November 15, 1862

At home in our dear cottage again. The trip back was difficult. The trains are full of injured soldiers and grieving widows. I rose up from my own desolation to give aid to some of the wounded soldiers. They are so appreciative of a kind word. I feel I want to help them in any way I can. How many kindnesses was Arthur shown along the way? His companions in the prison camp protected him when he was ill. They made sure he got food when he was too weak. They kept him as warm as possible when he shook with chills. And oh, those angels of mercy at the hospital. They washed him as tenderly as they would a babe. Cooled his fevered brow. Put pen to paper to let me know he was alive. Helping the soldiers in any way I can is a small repayment of the kindnesses my husband received.

January 3, 1863

We have had word that President Lincoln has issued a Proclamation freeing all the slaves held in rebel states. Aunt and I celebrated with a cup of cider. How I wish Uncle could be here to see this day. He preached so strongly and agitated for abolition so much, he would have been overjoyed at this news.

January 24, 1863

I am determined that I shall go to Washington to nurse our boys. Aunt is against the idea. She cannot bear the thought of my going. She thinks it inappropriate for one who is a widow for such a short time to be exposed to such tragedies as I would likely see. I feel just as strongly that my place is in Washington doing whatever I can to help our Maine boys. I cannot stay in South Bridgton. I will lose my mind if I have to go to one more sewing circle and be the victim of such sad, sympathizing looks. I need to take action, or I fear I will run screaming down the street. Then all will know for sure that I have truly lost my sanity.

February 27, 1863

Aunt says if I am determined to go to Washington, I must at least wait until spring. We have had such rows about my going. I am determined to go. I do not wish to upset her or go against her wishes, but I am compelled to go. A couple of other ladies will go with me, I think. That makes Aunt more amenable to the idea. We are at work knitting socks, sewing shirts, and collecting needful things for our boys.

April 14, 1863

Spring has arrived and just when I thought I would be leaving for Washington, Aunt has developed a problem with her poor eye. It seems to be the same ailment that plagued her last year. It hurts her terribly and much of the time she must keep it covered to keep out the light. It weeps and is red and irritated. She is not able to keep it open for long. I cannot leave her now when she needs my help. So I will stay in South Bridgton for now, even though it frustrates me. The articles we collected for our boys will go to Washington with some other of our Bridgton ladies who I intended to travel with.

August 14, 1863

One delay after another. I thought to leave in early summer, but it always seems like Aunt has some reason for me not to go. Now she says I should wait until my year's mourning has passed. I do not see what difference that makes. So many women are wearing black in these dark days. Surely my being a widow should not be an impediment to caring for our boys. I fear I will never get to Washington, and I do so want to go.

November 15, 1863

It has been more than a year since Arthur's passing. It is still so hard to fathom that. We had such a short time together that it seems like a dream to me. My time as a wife was so brief, and my time as a mother still briefer. I do not know how to feel. I am neither maid nor wife nor mother. All of that was swept away from me. I do not feel like a widow, but I cannot act as though I am not. I do not mean to dishonor Arthur's memory, and I would not displease Aunt by cutting up a caper as I did "when I was young." I am at a loss as to what to do with myself each day. My main tasks are helping Aunt with the housekeeping. Glorious occupation! Not at all! I know it is a help to her, and I would bear anything for her for the mother's love she has freely given me. Still, I long for a life of my own. Perhaps in the spring I will be free to go to Washington.

March 12, 1864

Poor Ansel Fitch is gone. He returned safely from the war, and he married Phebe Patrick who waited for his return all that time. But he was weakened by those terrible months of privations. He died of typhoid fever. Seventeen days after we attended his marriage, we buried him in the cemetery by the lake. His bride is heartbroken. She has not even a child to comfort her in her loss. Just two months later, his sister Cal died, too. When I think back to those carefree times before the war, I wish I had treated them with more care, as Aunt told me so many times that I should. Mrs. Fitch looks so old and drawn now. She has suffered such great losses, and my heart aches for her. It seems the whole town is wearing mourning and so many homes have vacant chairs. Will this horrible war never end?

April 20, 1864

At last! At last! I am on the train heading to Washington to nurse. I travel with two delightful companions from Bridgton. It makes it less lonesome and wearing to pass the time with good company. We are well provisioned with socks, blankets, bandages, and delicacies for our boys. Hurrah for Jordan and Company! Hurrah!

May 8, 1864

The wounded from a place known as the Wilderness flooded the hospital these past couple days. The wounds are grievous. Many are burned horribly. They say the woods caught fire from the cannons, and some of our boys lay wounded and could not escape the flames. I shudder to think of it but some of our boys who could not escape the flames shot themselves rather than be burned. Today's shift was especially long and difficult. I felt as though I was everywhere at once. I did not know how hard this work would be, and there are times I wish I had stayed at home. But then I see the looks on the soldier's faces. They are wounded and far from home. A kind word means so much to them. And verily I think they see us as angels. We go bed to bed, speaking encouraging words, offering water, giving a comforting pat on the arm, reading to them or helping them write letters home. I always seek out our Maine boys and give them extra care. Two Fryeburg men are in my care right now. Cousins John and Joseph Page. John has a broken leg, and Joseph has a head wound. I think they will both be fine. I think Joseph will be released soon. John says Joseph pulled him from the flames, and although they joke with each other as boys do, I can see they have suffered much.

May 12, 1864

As I predicted, Joseph Page has been released by the surgeon and will be rejoining his unit. Thinking his cousin would be lonesome without him, I stopped by John Page's bedside this morning to ask him if he wanted to send a letter home to his wife or parents. He said he had no wife but would relish sending his parents a line or two. I gave him paper and pencil and told him I would stop by later to get his letter for the mail. He asked me if I might stop with him for a bit to talk about home. We talked of our memories of Fryeburg, and I told him about my visits with my cousins and friends. Fryeburg is such a small village that it didn't take long before we found we had mutual friends. We promised to look each other up after the war.

May 30, 1864

As I write this, I am very weak. I came down with what the doctors think was typhoid fever. I have never been so ill in all my life. Martha says they despaired of my life on too many occasions. I can barely rise from my bed and then only for an hour or so. I am afraid my nursing days may be over. I can't say I am sorry to hear that. I have seen too much suffering. Too much death. Too much despair. I shall never look upon the mass of humanity again with anything but a strong dislike. How we have destroyed each other in such brutal ways. I can only think that the angels must weep. Cousin Pitt has been to see me, and he is making plans to send me home. I long for the freshness of the air and the peace of my garden in South Bridgton. I want nothing more than to see my dear old bedroom with its familiar windows looking out on the peace of that village. I think to ever leave there again would only bring me more heartbreak. I long for the neat order that my dear Aunt brings to all she does. I think I will sink into my bed and rest there for a good year. I want to be as far away from suffering and broken bodies as I can get. It is not that I lack charity. I have poured all my love into caring for these poor wretched boys. I am weary, so deeply weary. I do not think life will ever be the same for any of us. Too much damage has been done. Too many widows and mothers and children cry. What will become of us all?

June 8, 1864

Oh joyful homecoming! How sweet to see the sunshine through my bedroom windows. To hear the sound of songbirds instead of the groans of the wounded. How comforting to sit in Uncle's favorite chair and remember our family life as it was before all this horror of war. How sweet to sit at that old familiar table with Aunt discussing the news of the neighborhood. So much of the news is bad, though. I have lost some dear friends because of this horrid war.

July 8, 1864

I have had enough of the interminable sorrows of this war. I need to distract myself. As such, I have begun a newspaper. My new title is Editress. I will print all the amusing stories I can come by. And if I cannot come by any, I shall make them up. This village needs some lighter fare after so much heart ache.

I leave this week for a long overdue visit to my Fryeburg cousins.

July 20, 1864

I am stopping at Cousin Martha's. We have had a grand visit, going about seeing all the folks. As I had promised to do, I looked up Mr. John Page who I nursed in Washington. He is well-healed from his injuries and says he owes it all to my skillful nursing. He says my cheerfulness was a balm. He is a fine looking gentleman, but I think he likes to flirt with the ladies a little too much.

August 1, 1864

I had a letter today from Mr. Page. He requests Aunt's permission to call upon me. He suggests perhaps we could go for a carriage ride if the day is fine. I think I shall tell him yes. It has been too long since I felt a little young and carefree. Perhaps it would do me good.

August 8, 1864

Today I rode out with Mr. Page, and we had as fine a time as I have had in years. He is a handsome man and full of fun. He kept me laughing all through the village. I think he may have warm feelings for me. We spoke of many things, but on one topic we were both silent. Neither one of us brought up the war. For that, I am thankful. I simply cannot bear to talk of it. He has asked to escort me on a picnic next week. I think I shall go.

August 9, 1864

I awoke screaming from a nightmare just now. I hope I did not wake Aunt. It is the same nightmare I have had often since Arthur died. I dream I am being crushed and cannot breathe. I hear screams of wounded men, and I can smell the putrid odor of rotting flesh. I try to escape, but I am trapped and hopelessly struggling. Once I force myself to wake up, I cannot shake the memory of the dream. It is as though a demon possesses me.

August 12, 1864

Received a letter from a certain Mr. Page of Fryeburg. He wishes to see me when I go to visit Martha next week. I think I shall court up that old gentleman just to see if I remember how.

August 26, 1864

Well, my courting must still be good because a certain gentleman asked if he could give me a kiss. I told him yes, as long as it was a good kiss. So he kissed me, and it was. I do like him. Aunt asks questions about him and our intentions. I tell her I intend to kiss him again. She fusses at me to behave like a proper matron.

September 14, 1864

I shall be heading to Fryeburg to visit my cousins again. This time, Aunt insists on going, saying she wants to visit with Uncle's relatives, too. I think she goes to check up on John and me to make sure there is no impropriety between us.

March 17, 1865

Wondrous to relate! Once again, I have walked right into a trap. Mr. Page has proposed, and I have accepted. I suppose one can say I have not learned my lesson after the first time. Still, he is a pleasant man and seems to hold me in high regard. I expect we will get along just fine when we wed. He is anxious to set the day, and I suppose we should, though I do not feel the need to rush. I have encountered some jealousy from others. The war has made it much harder for women to find husbands, and Mr. Page is seen as quite a "catch."

April 10, 1865

The war is over!! Just yesterday, General Grant has accepted the surrender of the rebel general Lee! After so much time and so much heartache, it is hard to believe it be true. There are celebrations being planned all over town. I can only pray that now we will all be able to return to the way our lives used to be. I long for the old settled way of life. To think I once scorned the "matter of fact" common places of everyday living. Now I crave some steady, dull years.

April 15, 1865

I was stunned to hear that President Lincoln was shot yesterday on Good Friday. Today, we heard that he has died. Have we not all suffered enough as a nation? They say there is a manhunt for his assassin. I do not know what will become of our country now without his steady hand on the tiller.

June 24, 1865

My wedding day. Today, I will join my life with that of Mr. John Page for better or worse, as they say. I pray we will have more of the better than the worse, but life is unpredictable at best, so we shall see. Aunt insists that we will live here with her now. I don't think John likes the idea much. Aunt is getting even more particular as she gets on in years. I think he would rather go to Fryeburg to live. I cannot leave Aunt alone, and he will bear it for his regard for me.

January 30, 1867

Very early this morning, after a long night of travail, I gave John a baby daughter. I think he was happy enough to have a daughter that he did not mind not having a son. Myself, I am happy my babe is a girl. To have another son would only bring back all that I lost when William died. We have named the baby Mary after my dear lost sister. She is as sweet a baby as I have ever seen.

February 16, 1867

I feel differently after my baby Mary's birth than I did after William's. When William was born, I suffered so bringing him into the world that I think I could not feel close to him. I could not love him as I should have. I felt so blue and far away. I feared I was an unnatural mother. When he sickened and died, I blamed myself. I fear the same will happen to Mary. This time I will hold my baby close and protect her from the illnesses and dangers of this life.

Aunt is quite taken with the baby. I have not seen her smile so much since before Uncle died. She sings the baby the same lullaby she sang to me when I was tiny. It comforts us all. My little Mary has brought sunshine into the dark corners left by the war. John is quite silly over her and gets up during the night to bring her to me when she cries. She seems to be a sunny, content baby. She only cries when she is hungry and then only until she is brought to me. John says we are the picture of contentment.

Life renews itself, it seems. From the darkness comes the light. This new little life is a reminder of all that is good and sweet in this old world. My cup runneth over. I know Uncle is smiling down upon us with his eyes twinkling to see our little family snug beneath the eaves of the house he loved so much.

March 18, 1867

My Mary is sick with a fever. She cries without stop, the thin, mewling cry of a sick animal. I walk the floor with her, begging her to hold on tight. I promise her everything a little girl could want if only she will stay with me. Kittens, and hair bows, and pretty dresses, and picture books. I cannot bear the thought of losing her. I cannot bear another tiny grave. I pray without ceasing, "God, please. God, please. God, please." Aunt and John want me to rest, to let them take a turn, but I cannot. I know if I let her out of my arms, if I close my eyes, she will leave us. I cannot bear the thought of it.

March 20, 1867

Last night, my prayers were answered. Mary's fever broke just after eight o'clock. The fever flush left her sweet face, and she slipped into a restful sleep. John sent me to bed, promising to sit next to her every minute and to wake me if she worsened. This morning, she woke smiling her dear, little smile. She ate a big breakfast and went off to sleep again. God be praised.

May 18, 1869

It has been far too long since I laid this old journal aside. Aunt grows feeble. I have taken over nearly all of the housekeeping. Between that and chasing after my little one, I find myself too busy for writing. Today, I sit in the garden enjoying the sunshine for a little while. Mary is busy talking to the flowers and butterflies as her kitten, Puff, winds around her feet. It is a beautiful sight. Mary is strong and lithe. A honey-haired beauty with lovely blue eyes. She turns three this month. It seems hard to believe that so much time has passed since her birth. Her father dotes on her.

John has been troubled of late with bad dreams. He says it is nothing, and he brushes off my attempts to talk to him about them. I am troubled with nightmares, too. Mine are of the war. Always the same. I wake weeping, and John pulls me to him until I can return to myself again. We are a pair, both shaking in our bedclothes praying for the sun to rise.

January 11, 1870

Aunt has been quite low of late. She is much troubled by fatigue and uncertain balance. She fell in the kitchen yesterday. She has become quite cautious as she walks through the house. She has slowed down considerably, and although she does not complain, I can tell her hips bother her, particularly when the weather is damp.

She talks often of the old days when Uncle was still with us. She tells Mary stories of when "Mama" was young. She talks of Will and Mary and our family in those days. My childhood seems so far away after all we have been through. It is good to hear of those days again. I am remembering so many pleasant times. Mary asks for her favorite stories over and over, and it is a joy to see Aunt smiling while she listens to my little girl's chatter.

February 3, 1870

Aunt has been stricken with influenza. She is so very sick. Coughing, fever, chills. She feels absolutely miserable. More so because Mary cannot be near her. I have been making her recipe for chicken soup to help her get well. She seems a bit better this morning. Hopefully, she is on the mend.

February 18, 1870

Aunt seemed better for a couple of days, and then she got much worse. The doctor says her influenza has turned to pleurisy. She has such a pain in her lung that she cannot get comfortable. Her chest rattles with fluid. I am quite concerned for her. I bring steaming bowls of water to her room and cover her head with a towel so she can breathe the vapors. It helps her to breathe somewhat better. I begin to fear we may lose her.

February 22, 1870

Two days ago, my beloved Aunt died. I take the loss quite hard. She was all the mother I ever really knew. She gave her love to me not from duty but by choice, and I have always loved her for that. It was she who taught me to be a good, Christian woman by her untiring example. She was a helpmeet to Uncle in his parish work. Always willing to listen to him when he talked of his sermons or of problems in the parish. She mothered so many, without ever having any of her own. She took Will, Mary, and I in when we were young and helpless in the world. And so many others have come and stayed with her. I wish Will were here. I need his steady guidance. He is in the midst of a trial in Augusta and will arrive as soon as he can. His presence will be a blessing to me. I do not know what I am to do about all that needs to be done. This is the first time I will be responsible for making funeral arrangements and taking care of her estate. John does not grieve her loss. She did not make his life easy with her particularness. I can see the relief on his face even though he does not speak it out loud.

February 25, 1870

We laid Aunt to rest in the cemetery next to Uncle, Mary, William, and her sister Abby. I know she is with Uncle now, and that thought comforts me. I have lost my guide through this life. Although I often chafed at her strict rules, she was the only constant in all my days. One after another, all those I have loved have been lost to me. I am feeling bereft and alone in it. Mary is too young to understand, and John did not love Aunt as I do. How could he, having only known her during her declining years?

March 28, 1870

How strange it is to me to be after all these years, the mistress of my own household. Aunt has run this cottage so well for so long, that I feel a bit lost now that I must order my own days. I do not think I will change much of how things go. I am not sure what will happen now with the house. It belongs to Will now, but he has no plans to move here. His law practice will keep him in Brunswick, at least for now. Aunt left me a small legacy. John insists we will not live on anyone's money but that which he makes by his own hand. Will holds my money for me to keep it safe. Perhaps one day I will have a need of it, but for now what we have is sufficient.

June 14, 1870

John wants to move to Fryeburg now the Aunt is gone. Will says we may stay at home if it pleases us, but John is determined to go. He says his sister Abby needs help with the rooming house. I think we will go. Part of me does not want to leave home. It is the only home I've known. The rooms echo with the laughter of my youth. But another part of me feels the need for a change. These rooms also echo with the hollow sighs of all I have lost. Uncle. Aunt. Arthur. Our babe. All gone. I am so torn. When I look around these rooms I see so much of my life. The marks on the wall where Uncle measured us as we grew. Aunt's tidy kitchen where I learned to keep house. My bedroom where I dreamed of how my life would be. That same room I shared with my dear sister Mary, giggling and talking. Then again, that same room I shared with

Arthur in our early days of marriage. How can I leave all that behind? How can I stay? All of my family here is gone. Aunt and Uncle, Mary, and baby William all sleeping in the cemetery by the pond. My father lost at sea. My mother dead of a broken heart. So many of my friends dead or moved away. I have outlived so many of my dear ones. Verily, I feel far older than my thirty three years. So I think we will go. I would have my little Mary know family as she grows. In Fryeburg, she will be surrounded with Page and Fessenden cousins. And I will have useful work to do. John's sister is pleasant company, and she has her hands full with caring for her Academy scholars. Still it is hard to leave the only home I know.

September 25, 1870

Today, I attended my last service in Uncle's church. How many services have I attended there? Nearly every Sunday since I was a babe, other than during the war when I was away. That little church holds such fond memories for me. I know it will be my last service there. The new church is going up across the road and will soon be ready for dedication. It is a much larger, more glorious building than our little church. Plans are underway for a great fair at the Perley's farm to be held in the new hog house, of all places. I have made a good stack of embroidered handkerchiefs for the ladies to sell at the fancy goods table. It was work I did while nursing Aunt. Saying goodbye to this church and all those I cherish feels like a death to me. I do not think any other church will ever feel like home to me the way this one does.

October 26, 1870

We are now in Fryeburg in the big, rambling Page house. It is right on Main Street across from the church and the Academy. The street is far busier than what I was accustomed to in South Bridgton. John is well pleased to be home in the house he grew up in. I am pleased for him, if this makes him happier. Living with Aunt was not easy for him. She was so particular about how everything must be done, right up until the end. I know he bore a lot for me so that I could be there to take care of Aunt in her last illness. There is much I would bear for him.

Mary has her own little room close by ours, and she is much fussed over by her Aunt Abby, her grandfather Page, and the boys who board here. There are ten boys here during the school year. Abby is as a mother to them, having no children of her own. She makes sure they are well fed and properly behaved. She scolds them when they need it, comforts them when they are ill or missing their own mothers. When I look at their sturdy bodies and freckled faces, I wonder what my own boy would have looked like if he had lived. Some of the boys are about the age William would have been now. I find it hard to get close to these boys. I still feel so badly over my lack of love for my own. If I had loved him more, would he have lived? If he had lived, would Arthur have stayed home from the war? My life turned down dark paths when I carried William within me. I do not understand this still. I felt so gray and faraway after William was born. Like I was encased in a dark cocoon and could not be reached. I was not like that when Mary was born. I loved her and held her close right from the start. She was life and light returning after all the dark and difficult days.

December 25, 1870

A lovely Christmas celebration today. Some of our boarders stayed
on through the holidays, as they are too far from home to travel for
the day. Abby and I decorated the house to make it pleasant for
"our boys" so they would be less lonely. Mary follows the boys
about the house, prattling on about a hundred different things. The
boys are so patient with her, answering her questions and spoiling
her with little gifts and kindnesses. They are far from home and
missing their own younger brothers and sisters. It is good for Mary
to have older brothers surrounding her. They protect her and treat
her as though she is a beloved pet. We had quite a merry time
tonight. We ate a good meal and sang carols around the piano. It
reminded me of being home with Aunt and Uncle. This is my first
Christmas without Aunt, and I miss her so. It was a comfort to
have my Mary, John, Abby, and Mr. Page around me. I do not
know where I would be without their love in my life. We form as
fine a family as could be wished for when so many of my own are
gone from me.

November 2, 1871

John awoke screaming from a nightmare again last night. I tried to
hold him to me, but he turned away. He will not talk to me about
these dreams. I think he dreams of the war. I do not know how to
comfort him. This morning he went about his chores as though the
dream never happened. After the dreams, he is always short-
tempered. One of our boarders is sick with a fever. I pray Mary
and the other boys will not sicken with it, too.

January 14, 1872

A terrible smallpox epidemic is sweeping through this town. Many are sick, and we all live in fear. Our academy boys have all been sent home to avoid the contagion. I hear that Mr. Gordon and his family have all been vaccinated and are sick with cowpox. I do not know if I should have Mary vaccinated. There is danger either way.

August 30, 1872

We have had powerful rainstorms of late. During one, the Saco River rose three feet, causing much flooding. We are all as busy as can be with harvest and caring for our charges who are returning for school. John is much troubled by nightmares, and my health has not been good.

September 8, 1872

I walked Mary to her first day of school in the village. It is the first time I have left her with anyone other than family and close friends. As I walked her to the door, she kept glancing up at me, unsure of herself. I acted as though it was all a matter of fact occurrence, but inside I was just as nervous as she was. I walked her to her teacher, kissed her on the cheek, and told her I'd be back to get her when school was done. She looked so very small standing in the doorway. She was wearing the blue dress we made together for this special day and ribbons tied at the ends of her braids. I turned and left her there. I could not turn back to look to see if she was watching me leave. I would not have been able to go if she had looked the least bit sad. I will admit to a moment of weepiness as I walked back home. My baby has grown so quickly from the little one I held in my arms such a short time ago.

July 21, 1879

I resolve to write some in my journal and find I get distracted by the day-to-day cares of keeping house and taking care of Mary. She is of an age where her social life is all important, and we seem always to have bright young ladies under foot. They laugh and cut up capers that remind me so much of myself and my friends when we were the same age. They are good girls, though sometimes their high spirits get the best of them.

A delightful visit today from Mrs. Gordon. She brought some of her quince jam, and we shared it over tea. Mr. Gordon wants John to do some work for them again. It was pleasant for Abby and me to sit and chat. We don't often get to do that amid all the cooking, cleaning, canning, laundry, etc., etc.

August 23, 1879

A terrible day for the Page family. John's Aunt Betsey Page committed suicide by hanging herself in the barn this morning. She was about 74 years old and a very nice woman. No one expected this of her. She always seemed so cheerful. John went with Joseph to cut her down. A horrible piece of work. I did not want John to go because I thought it would make his nightmares worse. But he would help his cousin, so he went.

September 30, 1882

The Fryeburg Fair is in full swing this week. My friends and I have all entered something in the exhibitions. Julia Gordon has entered her quince jam in the jams and jellies judging. Abby has entered her bread and butter pickles. I have entered a custard pie from Aunt's recipe. We stand as good a chance as any other of taking a ribbon. Mary and Molly have been gadding about the fairgrounds, giggling, and flirting with the young swains. My Mary has my spirit, and she is a lovely girl. She is different from me in that I was always trying to send my beaus away, while she seems intent on attracting them. I find myself wanting to caution her about her lively, social ways with the boys, but then I hear Aunt's voice telling me the same so long ago, and I cannot bring myself to lecture her. She is a good girl, well mannered, and intelligent (like her Ma'am, if I do say so).

During Fair week, the men take some time away from their commonplace labors. They take some time to idle about and catch up on their gossip, though they don't call it such. They are far worse gossips than women. It's amusing to watch them each putting a boot up on a fence and swapping pitiable yarns. Still, they work so hard the rest of the year, I am glad they have a brief time to rest from their labors.

October 2, 1882

Miss Abby Page of this fair town has taken the blue ribbon in the pickle category! The competition was quite hot with many entrants. Of the many worthy contenders, hers were deemed most worthy of the honor. Alas, but my custard pie did not fare as well. Still, I think Aunt would have been pleased with the way it turned out. At least I did not enter one of my famous eggshell cakes!

May 22, 1884

My dear Mary has finished her formal schooling. She graduated with honors from the Academy, and I could not be prouder of the fine young woman she has become. We had a celebration dinner for her and for some of our boys who also graduated. The boys are all heading to Bowdoin in the fall. Mary will continue on at home, helping Abby and me keep house and tend to our boys.

June 18, 1886

I received a letter from Mary Jordan saying that her mother passed away two days ago. She was a good, Godly woman, and she was most kind to me while Arthur was away. She is another link to my past that now is lost. Mr. Jordan takes the news hard, and Mary says she thinks he will soon follow his dear wife.

December 17, 1886

John's father, Russell Page, died today. He was such a good man, and he suffered so much in his last years. I am happy he is at peace now. He was so kind and welcoming to me when we moved to Fryeburg. I will miss helping Abby take care of him. He was always ready with a smile and a joke, even when he was feeling at his worst. I know his care has been wearing for Abby when she has so many that need her care and attention. Still, I know she would not have traded the care of her good father for all the sparkling jewels of the world.

March 13, 1888

Since the death of Mr. Page, John has been sunk very low. I try to stay cheerful for Mary, but her father's uncertain moods wear on me. When he comes home each day, I do not know if he will be friendly or agitated. At times he just sits and stares out the window. We do not dare to speak to him at such times. I know Mary finds things to do outside of the house to avoid our troubles. I encourage her in that. She should have the chance to be young and carefree. I must always be vigilant to keep her from harm.

February 20, 1889

My "little" Mary has now turned 22. It is hard to believe that to be true. How the time flies by. When I was her age, Aunt was strongly encouraging me to marry and set up housekeeping. I will not put the same pressure on Mary. I would have her make her own choices. Still, I think she desires to marry. If that is her choice, I will support her in that. She is sweet on one of our former boarders who has gone off to Bowdoin College. Perhaps when he graduates we will see a wedding. I worry about her getting married. Although marriage can bring joy, it can also bring great sadness and many hardships. If I had my life to live over again, I think I would not marry. Still, I am thankful for my daughter. She has been a cheerful light on what is often a dreary path through this old life. I try to bear the difficulties with equanimity and a large measure of patience. I have Aunt's good training to help me with that.

April 4, 1892

Abby, Mary, and I set out early this morning for a walk. We aimed
to pay a visit to our Page and Fessenden cousins over near the
river. The day being lovely and the first breath of spring we've
had, we wanted an early start so we could enjoy as much fine
weather as possible. As we rounded the bend onto the river road,
we came nearly face to face with a spring bear. The glimpse we
had of her was of a thin frame with matted, scraggly hair. She was
by no means a candidate for Queen of the May. Mary stopped dead
in her tracks, and Abby and I collided with her from behind. The
bear must have thought us a fine looking bunch as she took off
running in the other direction. After our hearts stopped pounding,
we followed our own tracks back towards the main street to find
some likely gentleman to escort us on our journey. When we
arrived at the old homesteads, we regaled our cousins with our
brave exploits. We made many foolish references to each other
about how we looked as lovely as a spring bear, and so it went.

July 23, 1892

It seems this is more of a reporting of sad happenings rather than a
journal. It has been too long since I took the time to write in it.
This is a sad time for the Page family. John's cousin Joseph's
house has burned to the ground. Joe is distraught. He has had his
share of sorrow. His mother hung herself in the barn just two years
ago. He suffers from his war wounds, as well. I do not know what
he will do now. John had a nightmare again last night. He screams
so terribly, I am surprised he does not wake the boarders. It is good
we have a room on the back side of the house.

July 25, 1892

Joseph Page drowned himself at 4:30 this morning in Ballard Brook just below the bridge. John went to help Joe's wife and will stay there in her barn for a few days. I do not know what that poor lady will do. She has no home and no husband. I think losing his house on top of everything else was just too much for Joe to bear. I think he was never able to cope with life since the war. He is another one who never talked of his experiences. I think he was afflicted as John is.

October 2, 1892

A change has come over John since his cousin's suicide. I think he fears he will follow his cousin's lead. The nightmares come every night since Joe died. I have taken to sleeping in Mary's room since John will not let me near him when he has these dreams. I worry he will take Joe's path, and I watch and worry and do not know what to do. Abby thinks it will pass, but I am not so sure. I have seen so many of our soldier's come home changed after the war. The doctors call it soldier's heart and cannot do much for them. John grows increasingly irritable.

April 1, 1893

A horrible day. John went over to Mr. Gordon's to help burn off the south field. Mr. Gordon brought John home in a terrible state. He said when they set fire to the field, John began screaming and thrashing about. The boys tried to get hold of him to calm him down, and he landed punches on them, shoving them away. It took three of them to wrestle him to the ground. By the time they got him home, he had descended in to stony silence, and I cannot get through to him. He sits and stares out the window and shakes off any kind touch. I am afraid to let Mary near him, and I can see by her face she is confused and frightened by this silent stranger.

June 6, 1893

John woke the household last night. The nightmare again, but even worse than usual. He was screaming and begging, "Shoot me! Shoot me!" When I rushed in to wake him, he struck me across the face. I know he did not mean to, but I am so very upset by this. I have never before known a touch that was not loving. My cheek is bruised, and I try to hide it from Mary. She has such a solemn expression on her face. I am trying to pretend that all is well, but I am frightened by this turn of events.

June 28, 1893

John seems himself again. He has slept well for three nights, and I think the worst has passed. He had no memory of hitting me. He sees the evidence but cannot understand how he could do such a thing. It is not in his nature. How much our boys lived through. I cannot fathom it. I must help John in any way I can.

August 11, 1893

John has been much better for a couple of weeks now. I am finally beginning to relax again. I have felt as though I was keeping vigil. Watching over John to be sure he was well and protecting Mary from any chance of harm. I caught a glimpse of myself in the mirror today and saw the toll this is taking on me. I am so very tired. My dresses no longer fit me, as I have lost flesh from the strain.

November 30, 1893

Julia Gordon and her daughter, Molly, came for dinner with us. John was with Mr. Gordon, so it was ladies only. We had the best time fooling like we were girls. I was in a mischievous mood and got everyone laughing with my imitations of how men behave. I strutted about the room, hitching up my drawers, and pretending to spit out of the side of my mouth. I droned on about how the only proper place for a woman was standing by the stove rattling pots and pans. Oh, how we laughed. Our sides hurt so much we could hardly catch a breath. Mary and Molly, who are of an age, at first tried to hold themselves aloof from our foolishness. But, after a time, they chimed in with their own brand of foolishness, contributing greatly to the merriment.

February 18, 1894

Abby pulled me aside to speak to confidentially. I am so very embarrassed by this. She overheard the shouting last night and saw the bruises on my arm. She says she loves us both, and she knows that John has not been himself since the war. He has grown increasingly worse of late. Abby thinks I should go visit some family for awhile. She thinks time apart might help us both. I do not see how I can leave him. He is my husband for better or worse. And where would I go? So many of my loved ones are gone. I cannot stay, yet I cannot go. I feel trapped by this situation. If I go,

Mary must come with me. I cannot risk John's uncertain temper. If I am not here to protect her, I fear she will come to some harm.

June 24, 1894

We have been much plagued of late with deer in the garden. The woods are dry and the usual browse is dying back, bringing the deer into the village. They are lovely to watch from the kitchen window, but I think we will lose all of our greens to the voracious appetites of our visitors. The weather has been most dry and hot. Wells are drying up, and we have had several fires in the area. The hot temperatures make for short tempers, and we are all praying for a few days of rain.

July 19, 1894

My situation grows intolerable. I fear the setting of the sun because it means John and I will return to our room, and I will be alone with him. I try to be a good wife, to tolerate his moods, but I can feel how my spirit is sinking.

August 10, 1894

Julia has spoken confidentially to Mr. Gordon about my situation. I am mortified that my private affairs must be discussed by third parties, but I do not know what else to do. Mr. Gordon is writing to his family in Portland to see if there is a housekeeping position I could do at the house where they board. If I must flee from here, I must have work and a place for Mary and I to live.

September 4, 1894

I have left Fryeburg on the train. Mary is with me. We are bound
for Portland. Last night, John was sunk in gloom. Mary tried to
tease him out of it as she usually does. He turned on her quite
suddenly, sweeping his dishes off the table and striking her on the
cheek. He immediately was repentant. Crying and begging her to
forgive him. She sobbed in my arms. He slammed out of the house
and went to the barn, where he slept. He came to me looking
haggard and ashamed in the morning. He said he does not know
what comes over him when he gets this way. It did not used to be
like this. He knelt on the floor by my chair and sobbed as he does
when he wakes from his war dreams. He begged me to take Mary
away. Said we were not safe in the house with him, and he loves us
both too much to endanger us. He says he cannot control his
moods. A feeling comes over him like a raging river, and he must
get it out or he feels he will die. For Mary's sake, he begged me to
leave and take her away. It is as though a demon lives inside him.

Abby helped me pack our things, and Mary and I boarded the train.
John saw us off and wept as the train pulled away. Like so much of
the sorrow in our lives, I blame this on the war. It ruined so many
good men. I feel as though I am once again a widow. I do not
know what will become of Mary and me, but for her sake I must
do my best to find our way. I have the legacy from Aunt to tide us
over until I hear about the housekeeping position. I do not want to
spend Aunt's money. I would rather hold it for Mary to have
someday.

September 16, 1894

Mr. Gordon has helped me find a live-in housekeeping position at 76 Green Street, a boarding house where some of his family lives. It is not far from some of my Fessenden family, which is a comfort to me. Mary and I have a small apartment that we share. In return, I help prepare and serve meals, do laundry and cleaning. It is work I am accustomed to, and the atmosphere is friendly enough. I have led the other boarders to believe that I am a widow. To say I left my husband would only cause unwanted speculation and gossip. I hope someday to return to Fryeburg, but I can only do that if John's mind returns as it was. Abby sends us letters and says he has been worse since we left, but she is able to soothe him most of the time. He is working at odd jobs now. He is not able to continue working as a carriage maker. His temper is too unruly, and he sinks into melancholia so deep he cannot rise up in the morning. She says several times the doctor has been in to sedate him with chloroform to calm him down. I do not know what will become of him. I fear he has permanently lost his mind.

December 29, 1894

I am suffering from some sort of ailment that the doctors have not named. More and more, I am feeling fatigued. So much so that I have trouble rising in the morning. I ache so terribly that I fear something dreadful must be wrong. The doctor left me an elixir that helps me to sleep, but I do not think it does more than give me temporary relief. Mary has taken over many of my housekeeping duties until I am better.

March 6, 1895

I am maudlin tonight with the gray skies and drizzle of today. I am thinking back to all those boys I knew when I was young. I was so cruel to them. So careless with their regard for me. Aunt cautioned me over and over to be more considerate. She was right, of course. How could I have known then, how the memory of those young men would sustain me all these trials and heartaches later.

I was young and pretty enough that the boys seemed to hover about me like hummingbirds in a field of foxgloves. It was a plague to me then. I felt so pressured to marry before I was ready. And in truth, I blush to think of it, I was needlessly cruel because their regard made it easy to be. Now that I have indeed sobered down some, I see the folly of that. It was not the way Aunt and Uncle raised me to be. I was brought up on God's great rule to do unto others.

Tonight I am particularly thinking of poor Frank Wiggin. I treated him so carelessly. Although I did not want him as a husband, he was as fine a friend to Aunt and Uncle as one could find. He distinguished himself well during the war. Now, he lives in Aroostook County where he is a parson and a farmer. Uncle would be as proud as could be of him. I hear he married a fine woman and is raising a good crop of children.

How I miss those old days and the loving kindnesses I took so for granted. I did not know then how much a little bit of kindness could mean in this world. I did not know how quickly the sweetness of life could turn to bitterness. I wish I had savored the sweet more.

December 12, 1896

I pick up this book intending to write and find myself too weak and confused to put two thoughts together. The doctors have put a name to my ailment. They say it is neurasthenia. It is a common enough complaint. The only recommended cure is rest. It is said to be caused by having too many worries. I certainly have had my share. I am trying to rest as much as possible. Mary has been good as gold taking care of me. I fear the strain on her will harm her health if she is not careful.

April 22, 1897

I was able to sit up in a chair for an hour today with feeling faint. I think the rest cure and the elixir may be helping. Abby writes that John must be locked in his room at night, or he runs from the house screaming when he has nightmares. Oh, this life is so difficult and trying sometimes.

August 26, 1897

I asked Mary to bring me this book today. I fear I am getting worse. I am so very weak. Barely able to hold my head up. The pain in my joints is unbearable. I wonder if I will ever get well. I fear I will not. I think my time is short. I cannot bear the thought of leaving my dear Mary on her own.

Mary

Mary put down her mother's diary. Tears ran unheeded down her face. This was her mother's last entry. She had grown ever weaker, and two weeks later she was gone. Mary stood up, picked up her mother's tea cup, and walked to the tiny kitchen. Placing the cup in the sink, she leaned on the counter, staring out the window. "What do I do next?" she wondered. Wearily she turned and opening the door, walked down the two flights of stairs to the boarding house kitchen. Tying her apron around her waist she began washing up the lunch dishes.

December 6, 1899

A knock sounded on Mary's door in the early evening hours. Opening the door she found her father's worn and weary face looking back at her. Her reaction to seeing him was always the same. She searched his face to see which father he was. Was this the kind, funny Papa or the angry, troubled man who so often appeared? Watching her face, John Page could see her mixed reaction, and he knew his actions had earned her uncertainty. He smiled reassuringly and asked, "Won't you ask your Papa in?" "Of course, Papa, I forgot my manners." She hugged him briefly and took his coat and hat. "What brings you all the way to Portland?" she asked. "I came to fetch you home." "But, Papa, my life is here in Portland!" "Now, listen, daughter. Your Aunt Abby needs help with the boarding house. There's no sense in you being all the way down here being a housekeeper when you can be doing the same work helping your family."

Mary remembered her mother's cautioning words about returning to Fryeburg. Torn between honoring her mother's wishes and her father's request, Mary paused before replying. "What is it, Mary? I hoped you would see the sense in this plan. Your Aunt and I aren't young anymore. It's time you took up your share of the responsibilities."

"Ma'am wanted me to stay in Portland to work," she replied. "She wished it most specifically. And I have a life here. Responsibilities. Friends. It's where I want to be."

Her father began to get agitated. "I never thought I'd see the day when my own daughter put the care of others above the care of her own family. Your mother turned you against me with her wild stories, didn't she? She took you away from me. She poisoned you against your own father, didn't she?"

As he grew more agitated, Mary felt herself backing away from him as she had done growing up. When his temper rose, there was no telling what might happen. She remembered the bruises on her mother's arms and cheek. She cast about in her mind for a way to defuse his temper. "What would Aunt Abby do?" she wondered. Spying his carpet bag, she said to him, "Papa, you must be tired from the train ride. Won't you sit down? I'll make you a cup of tea. And then, you must spend the night. Tomorrow, we can talk this out in the morning and make our plans." She spoke soothingly of day-to-day affairs, asking about the home folks, until John began to calm down.

She made up her mother's bed for him while he changed from his travel clothes. She watched as he opened his satchel and took a bottle of chloroform from it. He saw her watching him and said, "The doctor has me take just a bit to help me sleep." Applying the dampened cloth to his nose, he breathed deeply and soon was snoring softly.

Mary sat watching him while he slept, wondering what the morning would bring. To return to Fryeburg meant she would become her father's caretaker, just as she had been her mother's.

Her father's uncertain temper meant she would always need to walk carefully around him. She wanted to help her Aunt who had been so good to her through all her childhood, but to do so would put her own health at risk. She desperately wished her mother was with her. She needed her wise counsel.

She slowly readied herself for bed and glancing in at her father saw the drugged peacefulness on his face. The only time he was free of his nightmares of the war was when he was subdued by the chloroform. She walked to the bedside table where he had left the bottle. Curiously, she picked it up, wondering at the ability of the drug to calm her father's worst fears. She carried the bottle and the cloth back to her own bed. Carefully tilting the bottle on its side, she wet the cloth. Climbing into her bed, she held the cloth against her face and breathed deeply as she'd seen her father do. She slipped into unconsciousness.

Dec. 8 1899
Fryeburg Record

Word was received that Mary A. Page, age 30, of 76 Green Street in Portland, formerly of this town, died on Dec. 6, 1899 from an overdose of chloroform. Her father John N. Page reported that he left her fine the night before. An interment service will be held at Pine Grove Cemetery on December 10.

April 21, 1904
Fryeburg Record

John N. Page, a lifelong resident of this town, died on April 19 at the Augusta Mental Hospital. He had resided there for two months after having been declared insane. He will be buried in Pine Grove Cemetery next to his late wife Phebe and their daughter Mary A. Page.

Epilogue

Cambridge, Massachusetts, 2006

Sitting in the sunlight coming through the windows in the reading room, she felt a current of excitement pass through her as the librarian placed the manila folder before her. Opening the folder, she found what she had come so far to see. She pulled the blue composition book towards her and read "The Diary of Phebe F. Beach, Esquire, 1857." She began to read the words written so long ago by a young woman whose personality leapt from the page as alive and spirited as she had been in life. Riveted by the story, she turned page after page until it was done. She heard the whisper rise from within the pages of that diary. A whisper that grew to a full throated song. "Tell my story," she heard her say. "Be my voice."

The History of Phebe Beach's Diary:

Separating Fact and Fiction

Historical fiction is, by its nature, a tapestry. Fact forms the warp, the structure, and interpretation forms the weft, the color and design that bring the tapestry to life. For an historian, the facts are all important, but for the novelist, weaving a story is paramount. This is the point where the two can be separated. Where the facts can stand alone making the historian more comfortable.

Phebe Fessenden Beach's diary is real. The diary covers the period of time from 1857-1862. The last entry in her diary is August 1862 where she reports the letter she received telling of Arthur's death at the battle of Cedar Mountain. The diary is preserved in the Women's History collection of the Schlesinger Library at Radcliffe College in Cambridge, Massachusetts. It is an appropriate resting place for her diary since Phebe was born in Boston.

The diary came to the library from a dealer in rare manuscripts. It was part of an estate sale. The diary was in a cigar box marked PENCILS. The provenance is not currently known. From Phebe, the diary would undoubtedly have passed to her daughter Mary. Mary's death would likely have put the diary in the hands of John Page and then his sister Abby Page. Abby Page never married and was cared for in late life by a local doctor. Upon her death, she left her house to the doctor, who later donated the house to the Congregational church across the street. The church used the house as a parsonage and then sold it. It currently houses a law office. It is not currently known whether Abby Page's personal effects went to a family member or stayed with the house.

Phebe Beach came to live with her Aunt Phebe Perkins Beach Fessenden and Uncle Joseph Palmer Fessenden in South Bridgton at a young age, before the age of four, and most likely as a baby. Her parents were Samuel Beach and Sarah Washburn Beach. Her father was described in family letters as having a "horrible propensity to intoxication" and had "another hateful habit, profane swearing." He was also said to tell "pitiable stories." He was described as "the lost one of the family." Phebe's mother seemed to have some issues of her own and was criticized for her behavior, although she seems to have improved somewhat after Phebe was born.

About 1844, Phebe's mother and possibly her father, stole her away from the Fessendens. As they came up over a hill in Sebago, the carriage overturned, and Phebe was returned to the Fessendens. The hill was known locally for some time as Beach Hill. Mrs. Beach's mother was a member of the prominent New England Washburn family, and they brought their full force against Joseph Fessenden to gain custody of Phebe. Public opinion was against Parson Joe because he was seen as trying to separate a child from her mother. The custody case was argued in Boston, and Fessenden proved his right to the wardship of the child. She remained with the Fessendens for the rest of their lives and was treated as a beloved daughter.

Samuel Beach eventually settled into a profession, becoming a sailor who was spoken well of by his captain. He is said to have died at sea. It is not currently known what became of Sarah Beach. It is also not currently known if Phebe had siblings. Sarah Beach was often staying with the Fessendens when Phebe was a baby, and they wished her to stay always with them. She may have returned to her family in the Boston area. The death dates of Phebe's parents are not currently known.

Phebe's first husband, Arthur Tappan Jordan was born in Denmark, Maine. He was the son of Mial and Mehitable Frost Jordan. He was descended from the prolific Jordan family, early settlers in the Portland, Maine area. Arthur's uncle, Leander Frost, was a blacksmith, and Arthur came to South Bridgton to work with him. There he met the lovely Miss Beach, as she recorded in her diary.

Arthur enlisted after the death of his infant son, William. He served with the 10th Maine regiment in Company C. He was reported killed after the battle of Cedar Mountain. A letter from Sebago, Maine from the Cole family was brought to my attention by Sherrill Brown, a Sebago historian. The letter reported that Arthur Jordan was not killed at Cedar Mountain but was wounded and taken prisoner. The letter reports that Phebe had refused to go to Arthur's funeral because she did not believe him to be dead. Upon finding out that he was indeed still alive, Phebe left immediately for Washington, D.C. The Cole letter was written on November 9, 1862 and reports that Phebe left "last week" for Washington. According to Arthur's tombstone, he died on November 2. It is not known whether Phebe made it to Washington before he died. Arthur is buried in the Soldier's Home cemetery in Washington, D.C. No actual letters from Arthur are known to exist.

The excellent regimental history for the 10th Maine, written by John Mead Gould, provided rich detail for Arthur's letters home. Also, Edwin Peabody Fitch's book *Ninety Years of Living* provided insights into life in the Belle Isle prison camp. Fitch was the brother of Ansel Fitch, one of Phebe's suitors, and Caroline "Cal" Fitch, one of Phebe's rivals.

In January 1863, Phebe wrote to her brother-in-law, William Jordan, serving in the army and at that time in Louisiana. She expressed her intent to go back to Washington to nurse the soldiers so that she could provide them with the good care that Arthur received. It is not known whether she actually went.

After the war, Phebe was again in South Bridgton and started a newspaper. She wrote humorous pieces, some of which are preserved in the archives of the Bridgton Historical Society. Her writing at that time seems to indicate that she is trying to put the war behind her and live cheerfully.

Some time around 1865-1867, Phebe married for a second time. She married John Nelson Page of Fryeburg. In 1870, they were living in South Bridgton with Aunt Phebe Fessenden and had a three-year-old daughter named Mary. When Aunt died in 1870, Phebe and John moved to Fryeburg to John's family home. John's sister, Abby Page, ran a boarding house for Fryeburg Academy students, and Phebe became a housekeeper there.

A record of John N. Page's draft registration exists, but his actually service is not known. He is not listed as having served in any of the sources found at the Fryeburg Historical Society. A John Page from Maine did serve and was a prisoner at Andersonville, but it is not currently known if this was the same John Page. It is possible he did not serve.

William Gordon of Fryeburg kept a diary, and John Page and other members of the Page family are mentioned often. John was a carriage maker, a painter, and a handyman. William Gordon reported Mary Page's death and John Page's committal to the Augusta Mental Hospital and his subsequent death.

In 1895 and until her death, Phebe was living in Portland at 76 Green Street. She was listed as the widow of John Page. At least part of the time, Mary was living there with her. John did not actually die until 1904. The facts seem to indicate a separation. It led me to ask the question, "What would cause a woman to leave her husband, move to the city, and claim herself to be a widow?" My conclusion was she that she was escaping from a bad situation. I could not bring myself to paint John Page as "merely" abusive. Instead, I chose to have him suffer from post-traumatic stress due to the war.

Phebe's cause of death was reported as "Neurasthenia." The symptoms of neurasthenia are much like those of the modern diagnoses of Chronic Fatigue Syndrome or Fibromyalgia.

Mary Page died just two years after her mother. She was still living at 76 Green Street in Portland. William Gordon's diary reported her death and mentioned that "Her father left her fine the night before." When I found Mary's death certificate, it reported that she had died from an overdose of chloroform. This was a common method of suicide during that time. It was also a method for murder. Did John Page have something to do with his daughter's death? It is an unknown. I have chosen to make Mary's death an accident because the alternative was more than I could bear.

John Page did, indeed, die at the Augusta Mental Hospital. He was reported in William Gordon's diary as having been insane for two months. His cause of death on the death certificate says "senile dementia." In the absence of fact, we all have to draw our own conclusions.

Phebe, John, and Mary Page are buried in the Pine Grove Cemetery in Fryeburg, Maine. Phebe's childhood home in South Bridgton still stands. It has been lovingly cared for with many historical details still intact. It is privately owned.

There you have my tapestry, woven of fact and fiction. Did I get it right? I do not know. I continue to research Phebe's life and hope to uncover more facts that will prove or disprove my theories. My greatest concern is that I may have painted John Page in a false light. I apologize to his memory and to his descendents if that is the case. The mistakes are all my own, born of not knowing what really happened so long ago. When Phebe was a child, and she committed a transgression against a family member she would say, "Forgive me and call me dear." I can only ask the same.

Caroline Grimm

Lark's Haven
Bridgton, Maine
2013

Voices of Pondicherry

Nestled in the rolling, verdant foothills of the White Mountains lies the village of Pondicherry, now known as Bridgton, Maine. Most of the early settlers of the town came from Boxford, Massachusetts and included members of some of the leading families of that area.

These settlers came to an unbroken wilderness and with determination, perseverance, and a strong faith in God, worked to wrest homesteads, shops, and farms from the forests. Dangers surrounded them, illness and injury stalked them, and isolation and loneliness accompanied them as they went about the daily struggle for survival.

Once the daily needs of food, shelter, and warmth were met, these pioneers turned their efforts to creating schools to educate their children and to building churches for worship. Town governments were formed to oversee affairs and sort out disputes.

Social activities provided an opportunity for neighbors to gather to discuss important news of the day—births, deaths, sicknesses, marriages. These social activities were the heart of the town. Skating parties, sleigh rides, singing, church suppers, swimming, taffy pulls, carriage rides all offered people a chance to come together and strengthen bonds.

Hardships were many. Epidemics swept through the town on several occasions, wiping out large numbers of the population. The Civil War claimed the lives of many young men and left heartbroken widows and mothers to grieve.

Despite the hardships, the town flourished and continues to flourish today. The modern day Pondicherry is a small town with a beautiful main street, and is surrounded by the natural beauty of lakes, forests, and mountains.

Many of the town's historic houses still stand; lovingly maintained by generations of people who respect and value the past. Graves of veterans of all wars are honored with flags each Memorial Day. In the midst of busy, modern living, the history of the town is not forgotten. There is a sense of pride and a determination to preserve that history for future generations.

The voices of those who have come before still echo in the streets, the churches, the gracious homes. And it is those voices that whisper of stories to be told. Stories that should not be forgotten. They are the Voices of Pondicherry.

For more information about the Voices of Pondicherry project and release dates for upcoming books, visit

www.VoicesofPondicherry.com

Voices of Pondicherry Series

Book One: Wild Sweeps the Wind

"I wish some great catastrophe would happen to somebody (not me, of course) so that I might have something of importance to set down in my journal." So begins the Civil War diary of Phebe F. Beach. Determined not become a "stocking darner and baby manufacturer," Beach spurned the attentions of every suitor who knocked on her door. Until one day, a blue-eyed blacksmith caught her attention and turned her life upside down.

Book Two: Beneath Freedom's Wing

Parson Joseph Palmer Fessenden was an ardent abolitionist and preached eloquently and often on the evils of slavery. His strong words led to threats on his life. Brother to General Samuel Fessenden of Portland and uncle to United States Senator William Pitt Fessenden, Parson Joe walked tall on a national stage while serving the daily needs of a small village church.

Book Three: The Old Squire

Squire Enoch Perley came to Pondicherry as a young man after the battle of Lexington & Concord. Working with his hands and his back, he wrested an empire from the forest. He helped to found two churches and Bridgton Academy.

Book Four: Cabin in Glory

Chloe Perley came to Massachusetts on a slave ship. There she was purchased by a gentleman who gave her to his daughter as a wedding gift. The daughter, Anna Flint, brought Chloe with her when she moved to a cabin in the woods after marrying Enoch Perley. Chloe lived as a member of the family and was the first "woman of color" in Bridgton.

Bibliography

Beach, Phebe F. *Journal*. Schlesinger Library, Radcliffe Institute, Harvard
University.

Brownstein, Elizabeth Smith. *Lincoln's Other White House*. Hoboken, NJ: John
Wiley & Sons, 2005. Print.

Coburn, Jacob Osborn, and Don Allison. *Hell on Belle Isle: Diary of a Civil
War POW : Journal of Sgt. Jacob Osborn Coburn*. Bryan, OH: Faded
Banner Publications, 1997. Print.

Dyer, J. Franklin, and Michael B. Chesson. *The Journal of a Civil War Surgeon*.
Lincoln: University of Nebraska, 2003. Print.

Eaton, Harriet, and Jane E. Schultz. *This Birth Place of Souls: The Civil War
Nursing Diary of Harriet Eaton*. Oxford: Oxford UP, 2011. Print.

Fessenden Family Papers. Bridgton Historical Society, Bridgton, Maine.

Fitch, Edwin Peabody. *Ninety Years of Living*. [Portland, Ore.]: Evangeline
Fitch Moke, 1976. Print.

Flagel, Thomas R. *The History Buff's Guide to the Civil War*. Nashville, TN:
Cumberland House, 2003. Print.

Garrison, Webb B., and Cheryl D. Garrison. *The Encyclopedia of Civil War
Usage: An Illustrated Compendium of the Everyday Language of
Soldiers and Civilians*. New York: Castle, 2009. Print.

Gordon, William. *Journal.* Fryeburg Historical Society, Fryeburg, Maine.

Gould, John Mead, and Leonard G. Jordan. *History of the First - Tenth -
    Twenty-ninth Maine Regiment. In Service of the United States from
    May 3, 1861, to June 21, 1866.* Portland: S. Berry, 1871. Print.

Krick, Robert K. *Stonewall Jackson at Cedar Mountain.* Chapel Hill: University
    of North Carolina, 1990. Print.

Joseph Palmer and Phebe Beech Fessenden Papers, George J. Mitchell
    Department of Special Collections & Archives, Bowdoin College
    Library.

Leisch, Juanita. *An Introduction to Civil War Civilians.* Gettysburg, PA: Thomas
    Publications, 1994. Print.

MacCaskill, Libby, David Novak, and Clara Barton. *Ladies on the Field: Two
    Civil War Nurses from Maine on the Battlefields of Virginia.*
    Livermore, Me.: Signal Tree Publications, 1996. Print.

McPherson, James M. *Battle Cry of Freedom: The Civil War Era.* Oxford:
    Oxford UP, 2003. Print.

Morton, Virginia Beard. *Marching through Culpeper: A Novel of Culpeper,
    Virginia, Crossroads of the Civil War.* Orange, VA: Edgehill, 2001.
    Print.

Pinsker, Matthew. *Lincoln's Sanctuary: Abraham Lincoln and the Soldiers'*

Home. New York: Oxford UP, 2003. Print.

Reed, Rebecca Perley. *The Story of Our Forbears*. Salem, MA: Higginson Book, [19-. Print.

Ropes, Hannah Anderson., and John R. Brumgardt. *Civil War Nurse: The Diary and Letters of Hannah Ropes*. Knoxville: University of Tennessee, 1993. Print.

Schultz, Jane E. *Women at the Front: Hospital Workers in Civil War America*. Chapel Hill: University of North Carolina, 2004. Print.

Shorey, Eula M., and Cara Cook. *Bridgton, Maine, 1768-1968*. [Bridgton, Me.]: Bridgton Historical Society, 1968. Print.

Sudlow, Lynda L. *A Vast Army of Women: Maine's Uncounted Forces in the American Civil War*. Gettysburg, PA: Thomas Publications, 2000. Print.

Varhola, Michael O. *Life in Civil War America*. Cincinnati, OH: Family Tree, 2011. Print.

Worsham, John H. *One of Jackson's Foot Cavalry: His Experience and What He Saw during the War 1861-1865 : Including a History of "F Company," Richmond, Va., 21st Regiment Virginia Infantry, Second Brigade, Jackson's Division, Second Corps, A.N. Va.* Alexandria, VA: Time-Life, 1982. Print.

ABOUT THE AUTHOR

Caroline Grimm moved to Bridgton, Maine with her family when she was seven years old. She grew up surrounded by historic houses, steeped in stories of the past, and her curiosity got the better of her. She immersed herself in local history for the sheer joy of uncovering the past lives of neighbors long gone. She wrote her first paper on the topic in high school. Since that time, she is often found haunting cemeteries, poring over fragile letters, reading crumbling newspapers, tramping across far flung battlefields, and traveling down forgotten roads. Her neighbors sum up her odd behavior by shaking their heads and saying, "She writes."

Caroline D. Grimm

BY THE SAME AUTHOR

Cash Flow Wizard series:

Stop the Cash Flow Roller Coaster, I Want to Get Off...

What Every Small Business Owner Should Know About Cash Flow, But Most Don't

Strength in Numbers:

The Entrepreneur's Field Guide to Small Business Finances

With Co-author Perley N. Churchmouse:

Dear Church Folks: Letters from Perley Churchmouse

God's Own Mouse: More Letters from Perley Churchmouse

Church Mouse Publishing
P.O. Box 605
Bridgton, ME 04009
(207) 515-0365

Bulk order pricing is available.